C000173946

APOCALYPSE 2000 - The Future ...

Patrick Heron is a graduate of Trinity College and has been a Biblical scholar for over 20 years. A husband and father, Patrick now runs a successful business in Dublin. He is always at pains to point out that he is not affiliated to any church or group.

'About the time of the end, a body of men will be raised up who will turn their attention to the prophecies of the Bible, and insist on their literal interpretation in the midst of much clamour and opposition.'

Sir Isaac Newton (1643-1727)

APOCALYPSE 2000

The Future ...

Patrick Heron

The Collins Press

Published in 1999 by
The Collins Press
West Link Park
Doughcloyne
Wilton
Cork

© 1999 Patrick Heron

All rights reserved. No part of this publication may be reproduced or transmitted in any form or by any means electronic, mechanical, photocopying, recording or otherwise, without written permission of the publishers, or else under the terms of any licence permitting limited copying issued by The Irish Writers' Centre, 19 Parnell Square, Dublin 1.

British Library Cataloguing in Publication data.

Typesetting by The Collins Press Ltd.

Printed in Ireland by Colour Books Ltd.

ISBN: 1-898256-76-4

CONTENTS

INTRODUCTION

The Book of Revelation is the last book of the Bible and is the only one that has not yet been fulfilled. It contains the prophecies of Jesus Christ concerning the last days of mankind and this earth as we know it. Many prophecies from the Old Testament find their fulfilment in *The Book of Revelation*.

The book was written by the apostle John on the Greek island of Patmos *circa* 96 AD. It has been called *The Revelation of St John the Divine*. This is incorrect as its divine title is given in chapter one, verse one, *The Revelation of Jesus Christ*.

The Greek word for revelation is *apokalypsis* which means 'to unveil', as in the lifting of a veil from the face. It can also refer to the removal of a veil in order to reveal the events of the future.

Many of the prophecies found in the Old Testament *Book of Daniel* are echoed in *Revelation*. After Daniel received these prophecies he was told, 'the words are closed up and sealed until the time of the end'. It is for this reason that few have been able to make much sense of *The Book of Revelatio*n for it contains many peculiar visions, images and phrases that have shrouded its secrets in a veil of mystery.

Although I have been a Biblical student since 1976, I, like most Christians, knew or understood little of this book. However, because I believe we are now in the last days, the veil is being lifted and the secrets are being revealed.

Suppose, for a moment, that it is 1912. You are walking down the pier in Cobh with a ticket that will take you to a new life in the land of promise. A stranger stops you and tells you not to board the ship because it is going to sink. But this ship cannot sink you say, it is unsinkable. The stranger says he has proof and pulls from his pocket a video called *Titanic*.

This book, *Apocalypse 2000*, is the book of evidence. This world is fast approaching an unprecedented time of holocaust and destruction. But the good news is, you do not have to go down with the boat. I now invite you to consider the evidence.

PATRICK HERON,
August 1999

Dear Reader

THE WORDS THAT YOU are about to read may be destined to change your life. I believe these words will be stepping stones by which you may pass safely through the flood waters that are beginning to rise around our feet.

The Book of Revelation is the last book in the Bible. It is the only one that is still in the future and has not yet been fulfilled. It contains the prophecies of Jesus Christ pertaining to the last days of man on this earth as we know it.

These pages contain a summary of many of these prophecies. There is exceedingly good news in the following chapters. In fact without a knowledge of the information which will be provided herein, many will have very little hope, as there is also horrific news ahead. However, if you can finish this book to the end, I believe your life will be enriched and blessed as a result, for it is written in the third verse of the first chapter of *The Book of Revelation*:

> **Blessed is the one who reads the words of this prophecy, and blessed are those that hear it ... because the time is near.**

Although from the neglect of *The Book of Revelation* one would suppose it said *'Blessed are those who do not read'*, since the blessing is so openly rejected.

These are the prophecies of Jesus Christ, the greatest of all prophets. This is the one book that Satan, the arch enemy of Jesus Christ, does not want you to read. For it chronicles his demise and foretells of his doom.

So this is a Christian book. In it you will get the Christian perspective. Some people may be offended by the opinions proffered. I make no apologies for this, as I am not ashamed of Jesus Christ and I am willing to throw in my lot with him. Let the cards fall as they may.

If you are a critic and you are reviewing this work, then know that this is a book on eschatology. More than likely you are ignorant of this subject. But, as Will Rogers once said, *'Everyone is ignorant. Just in different subjects'*. My hope is that you may be swayed, by the weight of evidence, to acknowledge the literary and academic merits of the Bible, the Word of God, and the prophecy it contains.

A preacher was once asked, 'How would you defend the truth of the Word of God?' After pondering the question he replied 'I would defend it as I would defend a lion in a cage ... by opening the door and letting it out'.

This is what I will endeavour to do in this message.

If you are already doubting the veracity of what you are now reading, I would urge you to put this book safely to one side, for very soon you may find yourself in the midst of the events that are about to unfold on this earth. In such a situation, the information contained in these pages may be invaluable to you and your loved ones.

The reason we are telling you these things are going to happen is so that when they begin to come to pass, you will know that we are telling you the truth, and that Jesus Christ is the key.

Proof o' the Puddin'

FROM AN ACADEMIC AND literary point of view, the Bible stands head and shoulders above any other book ever written, yet it is largely ignored in academia. It has sold over eight billion copies in more than 2,000 languages. It was written by 40 different men over a period of 1,600 years yet it remains united in its content. It has survived 40 centuries of history. It has more ancient manuscripts to authenticate it than any other ten pieces of ancient literature put together.

In fact there are over 5,000 Greek manuscripts of the New Testament, the oldest dating to around 68AD. Compare this with only nine old copies of 'Caesar's Gallic War' and the oldest of these is 900 years after Caesar died. Yet nobody questions these?

When copying was being carried out, the Hebrew scribes had enormous reverence for the text of the Bible. Copies were checked, double checked and re-checked many times. If a small mistake was made, the whole page would be re-written. When they came to the word 'Yaweh', meaning God, they would burn the pen and change their clothes. Only photocopying is more accurate than the methods they followed to preserve the accuracy and integrity of the text.

One would think that those who occupy the seats of higher learning would acknowledge the obvious literary merits of the Bible. It was, after all:

– The source of over 1200 quotations used by William Shakespeare in his works.

– The inspiration for literary giants such as Milton, C. S. Lewis, Sir Walter Scott and Charles Dickens.

– The inspiration for Da Vinci's *Last Supper,* Michelangelo's *Pieta* and Handel's *Messiah* which he wrote in 21 days, the entire text coming from *The Book of Isaiah.*

– The origin of hundreds of expressions such as 'render unto Caesar', 'let him that has no sin cast the first stone', 'all things to all men', 'a house divided cannot stand', 'salt of the earth', etc.

– The motivation for the work of Mother Theresa, Abraham Lincoln, Isaac Newton and Martin Luther King.

Yet despite its unequalled position as an academic document, the Bible is ignored and withheld from students of literary works. It is sidelined and boycotted and scoffed at in favour of lesser works of men. You would think that even the humanist non-believer would pay tribute to the academic worth of this mighty tome, and the effect it has had on the history of civilisation. But no, all are silent.

The difference between the Bible and every other book written, both religious and secular, is that only the Bible is prophetic. About one-third of the Bible is prophecy, i.e., foretelling events before they happen. Thus the veracity of the prophecy is either borne out in time or proven false.

No other book contains predictions about the future. For if they did, their non-fulfilment would have long since proved them wrong. For instance, there are 737 distinct prophecies in the entire Bible. Some of these are mentioned only a few times. Others are mentioned hundreds of times. Of these, 594 (over

80%) have already been fulfilled with 100% accuracy to date. The rest of these predictions pertain to our future.

In the lifetime of Jesus Christ, about 300 predictions were fulfilled which had been written throughout the Old Testament concerning his life, death and resurrection. It was prophesied that the Messiah would be born in the tiny village of Bethlehem (*Micah 5:2*). Prophecy told us he would be born of a virgin (*Isaiah 7:14*). *Isaiah,* Chapter 53 tells of his life, his death, his atonement and his resurrection. Isaiah wrote this prophecy about 650 years before Christ was born. In the last 24 hours of his life, 25 specific prophecies were fulfilled. All these were written from between 500 - 1000 years BC. Yet they were all fulfilled in one man in one 24-hour period. It was prophesied that:

1. The Messiah would be betrayed for 30 pieces of silver. (*Zechariah 11:12*)
2. Be betrayed by a friend. (*Psalm 41:9*)
3. Be forsaken by his disciples. (*Zechariah 13:7*)
4. Be accused by false witnesses. (*Psalm 35:11*)
5. Be dumb before his accusers. (*Isaiah 53:7*)
6. Be scourged. (*Isaiah 50:6*)
7. Have his garments parted. (*Psalm 22:18*)
8. Be mocked by his enemies. (*Psalm 22:7,8*)
9. Be given gall and vinegar to drink. (*Psalm 69:21*)
10. Not one bone of his body be broken. (*Psalm 34:20*)
11. He die with malefactors and thieves. (*Isaiah 53:12*)
12. The 30 pieces of silver be used to buy the Potters field. (*Zechariah 11:13*)

Even in his own life he made prophecies concerning himself which were fulfilled. Once he told his disciples that he must go to Jerusalem, suffer and die, and rise again (as the prophets had written). Peter rebuked him for this. He said to Peter '**before the cock crows twice, you will deny me thrice**'.

Subsequently, during the arrest and torture of Jesus, various people accused Peter of being with Christ. After his third denial the sun began to rise and the cock crowed. Suddenly Peter remembered what Christ had said to him. He wept bitterly.

If the religious leaders at the time of Jesus had known the prophecy concerning the Messiah, they would have instantly recognised him, because he came into the world with so many labels on him. But they did not know or believe the prophets and consequently they crucified him as an impostor (thus fulfilling those prophecies that said this would happen).

If the so-called religious of today do not know prophecy, then they will miss out on his second coming, just as the religious of his day missed out on the first coming.

Another quality that makes the Bible unique is its mathematical properties. The first five books of the Bible are called the Pentateuch. These were written originally in Hebrew. If you take the first Hebrew letter in *Genesis*, skip 49 and take the next letter, and repeat the skip sequence then every four letters spells **Torh** (the Hebrew word pronounced 'Torah', meaning 'The Law of God').

This holds all the way through the first two books of the Bible, *Genesis* and *Exodus*. When you get to the middle book of the five, *Leviticus*, it stops. However, when you do the same skip sequence for *Deuteronomy* and the *Book of Numbers*, it spells **Hrot**, which is Torh backwards.

Go back now to the middle book of the five, *Leviticus*, use the skip sequence again this time skipping every seven letters, and it spells **YHWH** (pronounced **YAWEH**). Which is the Hebrew name for God!

So we have every 49 letters in *Genesis* and *Exodus* spelling 'The Law of God' and pointing to *Leviticus*, and every 49 letters of *Deuteronomy* and *Numbers* spelling 'The Law of God' backwards and pointing to *Leviticus*. Every seven letters in this book spells **YAWH**; God himself.

Genesis	**Leviticus**	**Numbers**
Torh -> Torh -> Torh ->	**YAWH**	**<- Hrot <- Hrot <- Hrot**
Exodus		**Deuteronomy**

The whole Bible is a mathematical code making up an integrated message system.

Suppose you are asked to construct a genealogy of real people, but there are certain constraints. The number of words in this genealogy must:

- be evenly divisible by seven (with no remainders)
- the number of letters must be divisible by seven
- the number of vowels and consonants must be divisible by seven
- the number of words that begin with a vowel must be divisible by seven
- the number of words that begin with a consonant must be divisible by seven
- the number of words that occur more than once, must be divisible by seven
- the number of words that occur in more one form must be divisible by seven
- the number of words that occur only in one form must be divisible by seven
- the number of names in the genealogy must be divisible by seven
- the number of male names must be divisible by seven
- and the number of generations in the genealogy must be divisible by seven

Would it be hard to draw up such a genealogy? Well this describes exactly the genealogy of Jesus Christ as given in *Matthew 1:2-17*.

These are just a few examples to illustrate what a mammoth piece of literary and mathematical work the Bible is and that it is beyond the realms of human capability. If it is indeed God's Word and His way of communicating to us, then how does it authenticate His message? By prophecy, which is writing history before it occurs. Just as all the hundreds of prophecies thus far have been fulfilled with 100% accuracy, so too we can have full confidence that the prophecies concerning our near future will, in due course, come to pass.

> **For verily I say unto you, till heaven and earth pass, one jot or one tittle shall in no wise pass from the law till all be fulfilled.**
> *Matthew 5:18*

Here are a few expressions heard in everyday conversation which have their origin in the Bible.

1. Ye are the salt of the earth. *Matthew 5:13*

2. Ask and it shall be given
Seek and ye shall find
Knock, and it shall be opened unto you. *Matthew 7:7*

3. The first shall be last and the last shall be first. *Matthew 20:16*

4. The spirit is willing but the flesh is weak. *Matthew 26:41*

5. He who lives by the sword shall perish by the sword. *Matthew 26:55*

6. It is easier for a camel to go through the eye of a needle than for a rich man to enter into the kingdom of God. *Mark 10:25*

7. Do not cast your pearls before swine. *Matthew 7:6*

Happy 50th Birthday

THE TWO GREAT SUBJECTS of Biblical prophecy are the Messiah and Israel. Israel means 'called of God'. God chose the Israelites to be His people and promised that he would exhibit himself to the world via Israel. But today, 30% of Jews proclaim to be atheists. So how can God make himself known through the Jewish nation if so many say they don't believe in Him?

God can make Himself known to the nations by what he does to Israel. In the Old Testament, whenever the children of Israel walked in the precepts of God, they were blest mightily. No foe could defeat them. They prospered and grew rich. But God promised that if they strayed from His Word, then they would suffer the consequences of defeat and captivity. Time and time again the words of the prophets were fulfilled as the nation of Israel strayed away from their God and ended up in idolatry and bondage.

But what bearing does prophecy concerning Israel have on us today? In hundreds of passages in the Old Testament it was prophesied that the Jews would be driven out of Jerusalem and Palestine, that they would be scattered over the whole face of the earth, and that everywhere they would go they would be despised, hated and persecuted. Many of these prophecies were written even before God brought them into Palestine the first time!

In 70 AD, the Roman Emperor Titus was sent to quell the Jewish rebellion. He sacked Jerusalem and slaughtered about one million Jews. The rest of the population escaped and were scattered to the four corners of the earth. Everywhere the Jewish people have wandered, they have been despised and persecuted to this day. This persecution culminated in the Holocaust in Germany where millions of Jews were gassed by their fellow man. For over 1,900 years the people of Israel were in exile with no homeland of their own.

But other prophecies were given concerning Israel. It was prophesied that in the last days, God would gather again the people of Israel and establish them back in Palestine and Jerusalem. Around 1900 a few Jews returned, then more and in May 1948, the State of Israel was born. They have now celebrated 50 years back in their homeland. God said He would do this as a sign to other nations that we are in the last days. Today there are over five and a half million Jews in Israel. Even though they possess only one-sixth of 1% of Arab land, they are hated by all Arabs who are determined to wipe them off the face of the earth. World peace is contingent on what happens in the Middle East. Many experts believe it is only a matter of time before the whole area explodes into a nuclear war.

Why have the Jewish people suffered so much? Why is it that everywhere they have gone they have been humiliated and persecuted?

With the crucifixion of Christ, the sorrows of the Jewish race began, for when they rejected Jesus Christ they rejected their Messiah and they brought calamity upon their own heads. When they were baying for the blood of Jesus Christ they shouted with one voice:

> **'His blood be on us and on our children.'**
>
> *Matthew 27:25*

And ever since that day the sword has been upon the Jewish people, for God had promised them that His judgement would fall on them in the future Tribulation. But God first promised to restore his people to Israel and Jerusalem and that in doing this it would act as a sign to other nations.

> **And He shall set up an ensign for the nations, and assemble the outcasts of Israel, and gather together the dispersed of Judah from the four corners of the earth.** *Isaiah 11:11,12*

Bear in mind that this was written about 650 years before Christ. Yet here we are 2,500 years later and the Jews are celebrating their return to the homeland! This is only one of scores of Old Testament passages which foretell of the return of the nation of Israel after their worldwide scattering.

Scripture also tells us that when we see the Jews back in Israel then we are close to the last days. We can draw comfort from this, knowing that the good news is that our redemption is near and we are saved from the wrath to come. But first, the good news.

The Good News

I WAS 24 YEARS OLD before I realised what the year '1' signified – that our whole calendar revolves around the birth of Jesus Christ.

Christ's life was attested to by no less than 22 different historians of his day, such as Tacitus, Suetonious, Serapian, Phlegon, Lucien, Josephus. Many of these historians were antagonistic towards him, yet they recorded his existence. Josephus was a famous general in the Asmonean army and a noted historian of this era. He not only recorded the life of Jesus but actually wrote of the resurrection itself. And Josephus was not a Christian. Such was the impact of the life, death and resurrection of Christ that even secular historians of the day bear testimony to his work.

If the first coming of the Messiah was an important subject of the Old Testament prophecy, then His second coming is even more important. There are **twenty times more** prophecies concerning His second coming than there are regarding His first advent. From the Old Testament through to the gospels and epistles there are 318 prophecies concerning the Second Coming of Christ. In fact it is the second most mentioned subject in the Bible. So if the first coming of Jesus Christ is verified as an historical fact, then His **second coming** is twenty times more certain.

Paul mentions the second coming 50 times in his epistles, yet he talks of baptism only thirteen times. But what were we, as Catholics, taught regarding this momentous occasion?

> **Christ has died. Christ is risen. Christ will come again.**

There are two parts to the second coming. The first part is called 'The Rapture' by many Christians. This is when Jesus returns briefly to rescue those that believe in Him. The Bible teaches that one day, every Christian believer who is still alive, will vanish to meet Christ. Those who remain on this earth will be left to endure the holocaust of terrible events that are predicted in the *Book of Revelation*. But let us first take a look at the Rapture. Jesus himself first spoke of it in *John 14:1-3*.

> **Let not your hearts be troubled; ye believe in God, believe also in me.**
> **In my father's house are many mansions; I go to prepare a place for you.**
> **And if I go and prepare a place for you, I will come again and receive you unto myself; that where I am, there you may be also.**

So, we have this promise from the Lord himself that he is coming back to take us out of this evil world to a place prepared by Him.

As noted earlier, historians of His day recorded his existence. And even Josephus mentions the resurrection of Jesus Christ. The resurrection is the whole cornerstone of the Christian faith. Instead of gazing at a defeated, tortured dead Christ hanging on the cross, what should be on the altar is an open tomb with the stone rolled away and a notice emblazoned in large capitals 'HE IS RISEN'. Our victory is in the resurrection of Jesus Christ and what He accomplished by His death.

Many passages in the gospels relate to the risen Christ. Doubting Thomas after hearing of the resurrection said he would not believe until he put his fingers into the holes in His side and His hands. Jesus subsequently appeared to Thomas and invited him to touch Him saying:

> **Touch me I am not a spirit. For a spirit has not flesh and bones as you see me have.**

In *John* Chapter 21 it tells of His appearance to Peter and some of the disciples after they had decided to return to fishing. When they encountered Him on the shore, He was already cooking breakfast. So they all ate fish with Him in His risen body. He also told them that He would not drink wine again until we reach Paradise where we will drink new wine with Him.

Saul of Tarsus was the one God chose to take the good news of the resurrection to the Gentile nations. He had been travelling to Damascus to arrest Christ's disciples when a light from heaven shone on him and he was blinded. After three days his sight was restored and he preached of having seen Jesus. From that time on, he became known as Paul, who wrote the various epistles. Paul received many revelations from God. Here is his eyewitness account of the resurrection of Jesus Christ:

> **Christ died for our sins according to the scriptures, that he was buried, that He was raised on the third day according to the scriptures, and that He appeared to Peter, and then to the twelve. After that He appeared to more than five hundred of the brothers at the same time, most of whom are still living.**
> **Then He appeared to James, then to all the apostles, and last of all He appeared to me also.**
>
> *I Corinthians 15:3-8*

If you are an eyewitness to an accident or a crime, then you are a primary witness. So, according to Paul, there were over 500 primary witnesses to Christ's resurrection. And when Christ returns this will happen.

> **For the Lord Himself will come down from heaven with a loud command with the voice of the archangel and with the trumpet call of God, and the dead in Christ will rise first.**

> **After that, we who are still alive and are left will be caught up together with them in the clouds to meet the Lord in the air. And so will we be with the Lord for ever.**
>
> *I Thessalonians 4:16,17*

I know it sounds unbelievable that perhaps as many as 200 million Christians living today all over the world could suddenly vanish in the twinkling of an eye. Yet this is exactly what we are told will happen when the Lord returns briefly in the air. Let us look again at another parallel in Scripture in *I Corinthians 15:52.*

> **Listen, I tell you a mystery; we will not all sleep (die), but we will all be changed – in a flash, in the twinkling of an eye, at the last trumpet.**
> **For the trumpet will sound, the dead will be raised imperishable, and we will be changed.**

How fast can you blink your eye? That's how quickly we are going to vanish off this earth. Then the time called in scripture the Great Tribulation will begin to unfold. But the good news is, we will not have to go through this time of trouble, for we will have been removed beforehand.

The best testimony of the Word is the Word itself. He, Jesus Christ says 'I am the way, the truth and the life. No man comes to the Father but through me'. It does not say we come to the Father via your priest or your bishop, or Mary or the Pope.

There is only one man who paid for our sin and only one man God ever raised from the dead. That man is Christ Jesus and it is only through him that you have any hope. And it is only through believing in Jesus Christ that anyone has any chance of escaping the judgements and wrath that are about to fall on mankind and the world.

> **Since we have now been justified by His blood, how much more shall we be saved from God's wrath through Him.** *Romans 5:9*

This truth is repeated in other epistles. It is a bit like being on the *Titanic*. This is our opportunity to get off before it hits the iceberg.

There are no signs as to when the Rapture may occur, yet there are a lot of signs concerning the Great Tribulation, which lies ahead. However, because we can see many of the signs pointing towards the Tribulation, and we must be 'raptured' before the Tribulation can begin, it is feasible to suggest that the Rapture is close. In fact it could happen any time.

In the meantime, all we can do is watch and pray and wait for the Son from heaven who has saved us from the wrath to come.

> **Be anxious for nothing; but in everything by prayer and supplication with thanks giving let your requests be made known unto God.**
> **And the peace of God, which transcends all understanding, will guard your hearts and your minds in Christ Jesus.**
>
> *Philippians 4:6,7*

Synopsis of Future Events

I would like to present a brief outline of the events that are next to occur in the prophetic timetable. In the following chapters we will look in more detail at these topics and give the signs which we were told would precede these events. I will try to tie in events that are happening around the world and see how they fit in with the pictures we are given concerning the 'last days'.

These are the eight major events that are to occur.

1. The Gathering Together or Rapture of the Saints.
2. The Events of the Great Tribulation.
3. The Final Battle which Begins at Armageddon.
4. The Second Coming of Christ.
5. The One Thousand or Millennial Reign of Christ.
6. The Final Rebellion of Satan.
7. The Great Throne Judgements.
8. The New Heaven and New Earth.

1. The Gathering Together or Rapture of the Saints

The first event that must happen before the terrible times of *The Book of Revelation* begin to happen is called the *Rapture* by many Christians. Briefly, what this means is that the family of God, the Christians, those that truly believe in Christ, must be removed from this earth before the judgements of God begin to fall on this earth and mankind. Just as Noah and his family were saved through the flood and just as Lot and his daughters had to be removed before the destruction of Sodom and Gomorrah, so too the saints or believers of God must be saved from the wrath to come.

This is good news if you are a Christian. If you are not a Christian, or you are unsure of your standing, then by the time you reach the end of this book there is a very good chance that you will be sure of exactly where you stand.

Those of you who do not believe and are not Christian must go through the next phase of testing and trial. If you find yourself in this position, then do not despair, for there is still hope for you.

2. *The Great Tribulation*

Also known as the 'Day of the Lord', 'The time of Jacob's Trouble', the 'Day of Wrath'. This is a period of seven years or slightly longer when all the events prophesied in *The Book of Revelation* will come to pass. It is going to be an horrific seven years but many people are going to turn to God and Jesus Christ in this period and will be saved. However, many will be persecuted and executed because of their faith in this time also.

The seven years will begin with a tenuous peace which will be ushered in under the rule of a great political leader. The majority of the people in the world will give this man a mandate to govern.

He will be the most powerful and charismatic political leader ever to take office. Mr Clarence Larkin in his book *Dispensational Truth* says of this man:

> *He will be a composite man. One who embraces in his character the abilities of Nebuchadnezzar, Alexander the Great and Caesar Augustus. He will have the marvellous gift of attracting unregenerate men, and the irresistible fascination of his personality,*

> *his versatile attainments, superhuman wisdom, great administrative and executive ability, along with his powers as a consummate flatterer, a brilliant diplomatist, a superb strategist, will make him the most conspicuous and prominent of men. All these gifts will be conferred on him by Satan, whose tool he will be.*

Despite the fact that the world will love this man, and the Jews will trust and embrace him, he will turn out to be an evil dictator. His short reign will terminate after seven years in a place called 'Megiddo'.

3. Armageddon

Jerusalem is the most important city in Biblical terms and is called the 'Holy City'. It is also the centre of three great religions: the Jews, the Moslems and Christians all regard Jerusalem as their spiritual and religious headquarters. It is over Jerusalem that the last great battle will be fought.

In Northern Israel lies a valley called the Plain of Jezreel. It is also called the Valley of Megiddo because a town of that name is nearby. This valley historically acted as a funnel for travellers heading either East from Africa or Europe or vice versa for people coming from Asia and the Far East. Because of the mountain ranges lying to the north and south, the only way through was via the Valley of Megiddo. It is in this valley, according to *Revelation 16,* that the final conflagration will begin.

We are told that all the armies of the world will be gathered to this region for this final confrontation. These armies and the political leader known as 'Antichrist' will be met by another military commander who is returning this time to do battle. Jesus Christ is coming to wage war and there can be only one result. The first time Jesus came as a servant riding on a donkey. The next time He is coming as King of Kings and Lord of Lords riding upon a white horse and His garments will be stained by the blood of His enemies. Thus in this Valley of Megiddo will begin the last battle of our age known as the great Battle of Armageddon.

4. The Second Coming of Christ

When He returns the next time he is going to land in the exact spot where He ascended from, the Mount of Olives. We are informed of this in *Zechariah 14:1-10* which describes the literal, physical coming of the Messiah to rescue Israel and begin His reign over the earth.

> **Behold the day of the Lord is coming ... Then the Lord will go forth and fight against those nations, as he fights in the day of battle.**
> **And in that day his feet will stand upon the Mount of Olives, which faces Jerusalem on the east.**
> **And the Mount of Olives will be split in two from east to west making a very large valley; half of the mountain shall move towards the north and half of it towards the south.**
> **Thus the lord my God will come, and all the saints with him.**
> **And the Lord shall be King over all the earth.**
>
> *Zechariah 14:1-10*

Remember when Jesus taught His disciples the Lord's prayer? When He spoke this He was prophesying about the future. For you cannot have a kingdom without a king. When He returns as King of Kings, He will set up His Kingdom on this earth. It is only when this happens that 'thy will be done on earth', for His will has never yet been done on earth.

This quote from *Zechariah* is just one of the Old Testament prophecies concerning the Second Coming.

5. The One Thousand or Millennial Reign of Christ

After the defeat of His enemies at the end of the seven years of Great Tribulation, peace will be restored to this earth and the Kingdom of God will be set up under the rule of the Son of God.

Thus we do not go to heaven when we die to be with Him. But rather He is coming back to earth to be with us.

This will be a blessed time of prosperity, long life and peace for those of us who make it. We are told much about this in Old Testament records. Paradise was a place upon earth. This 1,000 year reign will be Paradise regained.

6. The Final Rebellion of Satan

During this 1,000 years, Satan will be bound, no longer free to deceive the nations. At the end of the 1,000 years, he is released for a 'short season'. During this release Satan goes out into the earth and deceives large numbers of people into a final rebellion against the Messiah and the city of God.

Even though man has been living and prospering for 1,000 years in Paradise, yet he again rebels against the Rule of God. Satan leads these rebels across the earth to once again attack Jerusalem and its King. But fire comes down out of heaven and utterly destroys the attackers.

Then Satan is finally thrown into the Lake of Fire where the Antichrist and the False Prophet have been for the 1,000 year duration.

7. The Great Throne Judgements

After this there is the resurrection of all people from Old Testament times. People will be judged according to what they have done. Anybody whose name is not found in the Book of Life will suffer what is known as the '**Second Death**' (*Revelation 21:8*).

8. The New Heaven and New Earth

After the 1,000 year reign and after the judgements, God Himself is coming to live and be with His family. We are told that He is going to make a new heaven and a new earth. Whether this will be a regeneration of this present earth or not we are not sure. But we are told that this present world will be burned with fire and a new Heaven and earth established. God is going to come to this new earth which will be the fulfilment of His Grand Plan.

Everything that has happened in the past and will happen in the future is but a preface to this main event. Then God our Father will have what every father wants, to share His love with His children who choose, by their own freewill, to love Him in return.

> **Now the dwelling of God is with men, and he will live with them. They will be his people and he will live with them and be their God.**
> **He will wipe every tear from their eyes. There will be no more death or mourning or crying or pain, for the old order of things has passed away.**
>
> *Revelation 2:13,4*

Just as over 80% of prophecies thus far have been fulfilled with 100% accuracy, so too these prophecies shall absolutely be fulfilled in due course. We shall now proceed with a more detailed look at the specific predictions given regarding the last days and the signs that shall precede them.

Parousia

Not long before his death, Jesus Christ sat down for a private briefing with some of His closest friends. This meeting took place on the Mount of Olives which is a hill just east of Jerusalem. They asked Him a very interesting question recorded in *Matthew 24:*

> **'Tell us,' they said, 'what will be the sign of your coming (Parousia) and of the end of this age?'**

I will now give you some of what His answer was and then I will elaborate on each point and tie it in with the prophecies of *The Book of Revelation*. These signs that the prophet Jesus Christ gives are directly related to the Great Tribulation period which is to last seven years.

Verse 4
And Jesus answered, 'Watch out that no one deceives you. For many will come in my name, claiming "I am the Christ" and will deceive many'.

Verse 6
You will hear of wars and rumours of wars, but see to it you are not alarmed. Such things must happen, but the end is still to come.

Verse 7
Nation shall rise against nation and kingdom against kingdom. There will be famines and earthquakes in various places.

Verse 8
All these things are the beginning of birth pangs.

Verse 10
At that time many will turn away from the faith and will betray and hate each other, and many false prophets will appear and deceive many people.

Verse 12
Because of the increase of wickedness, the love of most will grow cold.

Verse 21
For then there will be great distress unequalled from the beginning of the world until now – and never to be equalled again.

Verse 22
If those days had not been cut short, no one would survive, but for the sake of the elect, those days will be shortened.

Verse 24
False Christs and false prophets will appear and perform great signs and miracles to deceive even the elect – if that were possible.

Verse 25
See I have told you ahead of time

Verse 35
Heaven and earth will pass away but my words will never pass away.

(In *Luke 21* we have a parallel discourse where he provides us with some more predictions).

> **There will be signs in the sun, moon and the stars. On the earth nations will be in anguish and perplexity at the roaring and tossing of the sea.**
> *Luke 21:25*

Verse 26
Men will faint from terror, apprehensive of what is coming on the world.

Verse 28
When these things begin to take place, stand up and lift up your heads, because your redemption is drawing near.

Note this last comment. He says that when we see these things begin to come to pass, we are to know that our redemption is near. I would argue that all these things are happening right now. But let us take a closer look.

1. False Christs, false Prophets and Deception
Have you noticed lately how many weird cults or sects appear in the news? There are hundreds if not thousands of new groups sprouting up all over the Western hemisphere. Most of them have a leader who claims to have authority from God. All believe they have the truth. In recent years, many of these religious groups have ended in the mass deaths of their followers.

On a more local scale, there has been a huge increase in the amount of *'false prophets'* in our country. Every time you open a newspaper or magazine you have advertisements for personal predictions about your future from fortune tellers. You can phone in to radio stations with your personal problems and have a 'professional' read the Tarot cards to tell you how you might deal with your situation. Three out of every four people who pick up a newspaper in the UK read their horoscope. And now the latest gimmick is to invite your friends over to your house and have a fortune teller in to read their palms and disclose their past and their future to them (at a price of course).

Everywhere mystic and new age shops are opening where you can obtain books and information on all the occult arts and new age practices. From Tarot cards to astrology charts to birth stones and crystals. Again, this is a manifestation of the prevalence of false prophets and deception that we are told we would see as we approach the last days.

Nobody is teaching our children any alternative Christian doctrine. As a result they are lapping up this deception to fill the spiritual void in their lives.

We are specifically forbidden to have anything to do with fortune tellers, soothsayers, necromancers, astrologers and any other false prophets who are in total opposition to the true God and His Son, Jesus Christ. Time and time again we are warned of these people all through the Bible, but because we do not know these truths we are easy prey for the agents of darkness.

Suppose you wanted to know the future, and you were standing in a hall with two doors. On one door is the name Jesus Christ. On the other is the name Louis Cifer. Which door would you go through?

Most people I know have no problem going to fortune tellers, reading their horoscope or having their palms read. But when I try to tell them what Jesus says about their future, they don't want to know. In fact many get downright annoyed at me.

The first thing we are told to watch out for in the Tribulation period is people who claim to be true Christs and prophets of the true God. We were told when we see these signs begin to manifest themselves, we are to know that the time is near. Open your eyes. Look around you. The writing is on the wall.

2. Wars and Rumours of Wars

The United States have voted to increase its military budget. North Korea and China have the capability to hit American cities with nuclear warheads. India and Pakistan are now nuclear powers. Russia has almost twice as many nuclear weapons as the United States.

All over the globe there are wars breaking out and rumours of wars in scores of other regions. It seems every few months a new war breaks out between countries we have never even heard of before. And in other places, old adversaries are renewing their conflicts.

In verse 7 it says *'Kingdom shall rise against Kingdom'*. The Greek word for kingdom is *ethnos* from which we get our English word 'ethnic'. In other words one tribe against another tribe, which is what has happened in Kosovo and Rwanda.

In almost every country in the world there is potential for blood-letting on a huge scale. In South Africa, there are an average of 64 murders per day. In Ireland, in 1998, there were 49 murders. During the seven years of Tribulation I believe this potential will be realised on a wide front.

The time is short. We must take the time that is left to educate our fellow man in these warnings and teach one another the way of peace. It is only when individuals make their peace with Jesus Christ, who is the Prince of Peace, that a real peace will prevail.

We see wars and rebellion and contentions breaking out in our newspapers and on our TV sets on a daily basis. All these are mere portents of the last great war that will be fought at the end of the seven years of the Great Tribulation. We were told that when we see all these things begin to come to pass, it will be like the beginning of labour pains. As the birth gets closer, the intensity of the pains increases. You will see more and more wars and potential for war between more nations. You will see more 'ethnic cleansing' between tribes of people. All these things must come to pass.

There is an old adage that says *'The history of the World is the history of War'*. It is only recently I came to understand this proverb. Look at the pages of history. They are filled, from earliest days, with the accounts of battles and triumphs of one army over another. Ever since Cain slew his brother Abel, man has continuously gone to war with his neighbour. They say each generation must make its own mistakes. It is only just over 50 years since the last world war. They said the first World War was the war to end all wars. How little they know. In verse 22 of *Matthew 24* Jesus said that '**unless those days are shortened, no flesh would be saved**'. It is only in these latter years that countries possess the fire power to wipe all living persons off the face of the earth. If we don't learn from history, we are bound to repeat it.

3. Earthquakes, Famines and Pestilences
Earthquakes have been increasing in frequency and in strength every decade since records began in the late 1800s. Up to the 1950s, there were an average of two to four per decade. In the 1960s, there were 13 major earthquakes. In the 1970s, there were 51; in the 1980s, 86. And from 1990-1996 there were over 150 major earthquakes. This is according to the geological survey in Boulder, Colorado. These are official figures.

Along with earthquakes we are told people will be **perplexed with the roaring and tossing of the seas**. I believe Jesus was referring to an increase in strange weather. For to have seas roaring and tossing, you have to have strong winds. Record winds of 111 miles per hour were recorded over Christmas 1998. Never before have winds of this ferocity been experienced in Ireland. They left floods and devastation in their wake. Storm after storm has battered the coast. Thousands were left without electricity and huge areas were flooded. Global warming is being blamed for the peculiar weather we are experiencing in every quarter of the world. Tornadoes and hurricanes rip through towns and villages leaving havoc, devastation and death in their wake. Freak waves wash over low-lying land and drown thousands. Floods are occurring the likes of which have never been witnessed in living memory and leaving millions of people displaced. In every country in the world the weather patterns are changing. The polar ice caps have melted and receded by 150 miles in the last ten years. The hole in the ozone layer is now as big as the whole of North America including Canada. Even if we wanted to do something to reverse this trend, we could not.

An environmental agency said recently that in the last 30 years we have used up 30% of the world's resources. From fish stocks to the rain forests to polluting everything we touch. And now we are beginning to pay the price. Scientists tell us that when the next few volcanoes blow, the dust and smoke from them will blot out the sun and cause major pollution world-wide. And it's not a matter of 'if' but 'when'. There are 550 active volcanoes being monitored around the world today.

When it comes to famines and pestilences, it is the same story. Famine is increasing around the world despite the fact that there is over production of food in the developed world. One would think that in these days of fibre optics, cyber space and the internet, that we could have figured out how to feed hungry people. At a time when famines are continuing to flourish in the Third World, our farmers are being put off the land at the rate of 120 per week. And this pattern is being repeated worldwide. Is this a coincidence, or is there an agenda at work here? Jesus told us there would be a huge increase in pestilences (diseases) in the last days. It is hard to know where to start, for almost on a weekly basis we hear of new, stronger viruses and discover new forms of germs which seem immune to vaccines.

Despite medical advances, old diseases, once thought conquered, are making a comeback and killing millions again. Cholera and malaria are examples of these. Tuberculosis is another disease that we thought was under control. Now 3 million per year are dying from TB and experts at a World Health Organisation meeting said that unless action is taken, a billion more people will become infected and 70 million die by the year 2020. Heroin and crack addiction are other forms of pestilence which stalk our cities sucking life from our young people. And then there is Aids.

In South Africa alone there are two and a half million people with full-blown Aids. One thousand per day are contracting this disease. And this is the same story in every country in Africa. In some villages there are only old men and young boys to be found.

Does the rest of the civilised world care? I spoke to a man who works in the Dáil who told me that he saw a document that was produced by some world organisation. It was inviting other countries to repatriate Africa after it had been decimated by famine and disease.

An eminent scientist, Professor Richard Lucey, said: *'If CJD does, as I predict, turn into a full blown plague, it will make the Aids epidemic look like a common cold.'* Increase in diseases is yet another prophecy made almost 2,000 years ago that we are witnessing coming to pass before our very eyes. We are told that when we see these things begin to come to pass, we are to:

> **Stand up and lift your heads, because your redemption is drawing near.** *Luke 21:28*

Do you know what it is to redeem something? If somebody puts something in the pawn shop, say a watch, they get a ticket. When they return with the money they can redeem the watch.

Well, Jesus Christ paid the price for us with His death on the cross. He bought our freedom and the price He paid was His blood. He redeemed us by paying the ultimate price. No one else could have qualified to do this, for only He had no sin. Therefore His blood was sufficient to wipe away our sins.

He became the sacrificial lamb for all mankind. That is why when John the Baptist saw him he said:

> **Behold the Lamb of God, who takes away the sin of the World.**

Because of His life, His death and His resurrection we are

redeemed, bought back, out of the pawn shop of the devil. All you have to do is believe in what he did for you. It is a free gift to you. You did not earn it, neither do you deserve it, for it is a gift of grace. Grace means 'divine favour'.

When next your mind is filled with images of war, of famine, of diseases and of great physical calamities brought into your front room via TV, remember, your redemption is near.

The Land of Sinners and Perverts

TO SAY THAT IRELAND is a Christian country is a misnomer. Any vestiges of Christianity are fast disappearing to be replaced with neo-paganism. We are in a post-Christian era and our moral values have descended accordingly.

When describing the moral and spiritual state of the world of the last days, Jesus compared it to two other distinct periods of history. Firstly, he said it would be like the days of Noah when all the people of the world were '**eating, drinking, marrying and giving in marriage**'. The other time he compared it with was the days of Lot when he lived in the cities of Sodom and Gomorrah. Let us take a closer look at these two scenarios and see if we notice anything unusual about them:

> **Just as it was in the day of Noah, so shall it be also in the day of the Son of Man. People were eating, drinking, marrying and being given in marriage up to the day Noah entered the Ark. Then, the flood came and destroyed them all.**
> **It was the same in the days of Lot. People were eating and drinking, buying and selling, planting and building.**
> **But the day Lot left Sodom, fire and sulphur rained down from heaven and destroyed them all.**
> **It will be just like this on the day the Son of Man is revealed.**
>
> *Jesus Christ Luke 17:26-30*

The background to the time of Noah is found in *Genesis*

chapter six. It says that in those days the number of people living on the earth had increased greatly. But they had also increased in violence and immorality. Then it says that they were *'eating, drinking, marrying and giving in marriage'*. The implication is that this was their main activity in life – to eat well and get drunk – to fulfil the lusts of the flesh.

From a brief study of these few chapters in *Genesis*, we see that the people of the world at that time had descended almost to the level of animals. As part of their religious practice they used to burn their own children in sacrifice to their pagan gods. They had degenerated to the level of wild savages to such a degree that we are told:

> **The Lord saw how great man's wickedness on the earth had become, and that every inclination of the thoughts of his heart was only evil all the time.** *Genesis 6:5*

This is why God's judgement fell on the world at this time. Only Noah and his wife, their three sons and their wives were saved from the destruction which ensued. God gave Noah the instruction to build the Ark and fill it with animals. He was building the Ark for a long time, maybe 70 years, before the flood came. All this time the people around him were laughing at him building this huge vessel, while nobody had ever seen rain before, let alone a flood. So they continued on in the same manner of life. But then one day, when they least expected it, the fountains of the deep were broken up and the floodgates of the heavens were opened and it began to pour.

Every person, animal and bird were drowned. The whole earth was engulfed by this cataclysmic deluge. The floods continued for 150 days before it began to recede. It was almost a year later before Noah and his family landed and got off the Ark. We are told that 'as it was, so shall it be'. When the conditions that prevailed in the days of Noah are repeated, this will indicate the nearness of the second coming.

Likewise in the days of Lot when he lived with his wife and

two daughters in the city of Gomorrah. The conditions there bore a striking similarity to the conditions of Noah's day. Let's take a look at the background to his situation:

> **The two angels arrived at Sodom in the evening, and Lot was sitting in the gateway of the city. When he saw them he got up to meet them and bowed down with his face to the ground.**
> **'My Lords,' he said, 'please turn aside to your servant's house. You can wash your feet and spend the night and then go on your way early in the morning.'**
> **Before they had gone to bed, all the men from every part of the city of Sodom – both young and old – surrounded the house.**
> **They called to Lot 'where are the men who came to you tonight? Bring them out to us so that we can have sex with them.'**
>
> *Genesis 19:1,2,4,5*

The story goes on to show that in order to stave off the men and boys of Sodom, Lot offered them his two daughters. But they were not interested in his daughters. They wanted the two men. So they threatened Lot but the angels pulled him back into the house and struck the men with blindness. Then they told Lot to come with his wife and two daughters and escape into the mountains because God was going to destroy the city and the other towns around the plain. They were instructed not to stop and not to look back. As they escaped God rained down burning sulphur on Sodom and Gomorrah. Lot's wife looked back and turned into a pillar of salt.

So the conditions were the same in the life of Lot as they were at the time of Noah. And so shall it be in the latter days before the second advent of Jesus Christ.

> **It was the same in the days of Lot. People were eating and drinking, buying and selling, planting and building.**
>
> *Jesus Christ Luke 17:28*

The inference from this was that they were good days economically. People lived to enjoy food and drink. There was lots of profitable economic activity which meant a lot of building and planting of food. People were well off. This gave them ample time to enjoy the finer things of life – art, gourmet food and the best wines. And we are then told that 'all of the men of Sodom, both young and old' came around to Lot's house because they wanted to rape the two men he was lodging.

Homosexuality in the Bible is a vile sin. And it was because of this rampant promiscuity that God destroyed Sodom and Gomorrah and the towns around them. We read that:

> **The Lord said: 'The outcry against Sodom and Gomorrah is so great and their sin so grievous ...'** *Genesis 18:20*

The moral conditions of these two events, the flood of Noah and the destruction of Sodom and Gomorrah are examples of the coming judgement upon the earth as recorded in *The Book of Revelation*. Because of man's rejection of God and of his Messiah, the wrath of God will fall once again on mankind. But just as Noah and his family were taken out before the flood and Lot and his family were removed before the burning sulphur fell on Sodom and Gomorrah, so too the people of God will be removed when Jesus comes back briefly in the clouds to 'Rapture' his own. Thus, those of us who wish to believe God and accept his Son as our Lord and Saviour will be saved from the wrath and the Great Tribulation that will fall suddenly on those who least expect it. Paul, speaking of these last days, says:

> **For when they shall say, 'peace and safety', then sudden destruction will come upon them, as labour pains on a pregnant woman, and they will not escape.** *I Thessalonians 5:3*

Is there not a striking similarity between the conditions that prevailed in the days of Noah and Lot and the conditions of the world today? They were well off. Business was good. Economic activity was flourishing. The building and construction industry was prospering. There was over production of food with lots to eat. Consequently people did not have to work too hard as there was plenty of food and money to go around. There was also widespread violence. The pursuit of pleasure was their main objective and homosexual activity and immorality was the ultimate pursuit.

Today we are constantly bombarded by the liberal secular humanist agenda telling us that if it feels good, do it. Films, magazines and TV are continually pushing the 'free sex for all' agenda. Thus all the attendant ills that accompany these sins are prevalent. Divorce is rising everywhere. Sexually transmitted diseases are rampant. It is the same with homosexual and lesbian culture. And for the most part the majority of young people today accept homesexual practice as being normal.

From a biblical point of view it is not normal. As one biblical scholar, Mr M. R. de Haan wrote, 'Sodom has for centuries been associated with the most debasing, violent, most repulsive of all forms of immorality. The sin of sodomy above all sins causes decent people to recoil in horror and disgust.'

In Britain the government has reduced the age of consent for homosexual behaviour to sixteen. And the campaign continues to have the concensual age reduced further as in Holland, where the age of consent is twelve.

But Jesus Christ did away with the Old Testament laws and introduced a new era of love and grace and mercy. Today all sinners have the opportunity to turn from their sin and receive the free gift of grace and eternal life. In the New Testament Paul, regarding homosexuality, writes:

> **Because of this, God gave them over to shameful lusts. Even their women exchanged natural relations for unnatural ones.**
> **In the same way the men also abandoned natural relations with women and were inflamed with lust for one another.**
> **Men committed indecent acts with other men, and received in themselves the due penalty for their perversion.**
>
> *Romans 1:26,27*

This is God's view. I did not write the Bible. But as a Christian I am bound by my conscience to uphold what I believe. I would ask people with opposing views to be tolerant of the Christian position. After all, we are constantly being asked to be tolerant of the homosexual community. Why cannot people be tolerant to the Christian viewpoint?

I do not wish to harm any person with an opposing view to mine. We are all sinners and we all fall short of the calling of God. I am a sinner and no one knows that more than myself. 'God loves the sinner but He hates the sin.' Jesus Christ died for all men. Everyone can be saved and receive the free gift of God if they so choose. Remember Mary Magdalene? She was caught in adultery, the penalty for which was death. Yet Jesus said 'Neither do I condemn thee. Go thy way and sin no more'. He did not condemn her. In fact she became one of his closest friends and was at the foot of the cross with the other women when his disciples were missing. But he also said to her 'Sin no more'. He did not say she should go back to her adulterous ways. In another passage we are told he cast seven devils out of her, but he still loved her.

It seems that the media are always ready to promote anti-Christian principles. Mr Gerry Ryan had the leader of the white witches in Ireland on the national airwaves. She boasted of the 3,500 white witches in Ireland and 25,000 in Great Britain and Ireland. She got about twenty minutes of free promotion for white witchcraft with no difficult questions coming from the host. She also spoke of the many black witches operating in our midst and how they can do harm. But white witches only do good! Sure. If you have a can with beans in it and you put a label on it that says 'peas', does it change the beans on the inside?

All witchcraft involves Satan worship. One of Satan's names is the 'deceiver' and he is surely finding it easy to deceive.

Many media presenters would regard me as just another Bible-thumping fanatic. Another born again fundamentalist. Is it not amazing that you will never hear those poeple offend other minority groups, but you can slag off a Christian until you are blue in the face. We are ridiculaed, scoffed at, laughed at and ignored. And as time goes on you will see more and more persecution of Christians and you will witness more anti-Christian bigotry of this type.

Let me say to our media gurus that if St Patrick was around today, you would ignore him and slag him off as a fundamentalist (because he was). So were Matthew, Mark, Luke and John. St Paul was a fundamentalist as was Jesus Christ himself. And even though you might think you are safe, let me quote something which may have escaped your notice:

> **Many will say to me on that day Lord, Lord, did we not prophecy in your name, and in your name drive out demons and perform many miracles?**
> **Then I will tell them plainly 'I never knew you. Away from me you evil doers'.** *Matthew 7:22, 23*

Ah well, a prophet is not without honour, except in his own town and his own house.

In conclusion:
'As it was then, so shall it be.' This is what Jesus told us to watch out for almost 2,000 years ago. When we see the same conditions prevailing in the world as those of the days of Noah and Lot, we are to know that the day is at hand.

Because of the immoral state of the people, God made a judgement against them. He did this as an example to us. In both instances he removed the righteous people before he destroyed the rest. The immorality and perversion of our world today is a mirror image of the days of Noah and Lot. The earth is ripening for judgement. The day is at hand. It is make up your mind time. The choice is yours.

The Devil's Advocate

OF COURSE 'THE RAPTURE' is not a new concept in the Bible. Enoch was 'taken' by God and apparently did not die. So too, Elijah was taken up to heaven 'by chariots' so that he did not see death (*II Kings 2:11*). In the gospel period Jesus Christ Himself was taken up:

> **After He said this, He was taken up before their very eyes, and a cloud hid Him from their sight.**
> **They were looking intently up into the sky as he was going, when suddenly two men dressed in white stood beside them.**
> **'Men of Galilee', they said, 'why do you stand here looking into the sky? This same Jesus who has been taken from you into heaven, will come back in the same way you have seen Him go into heaven'.** *Book of Acts 1:9-11*

In chapter eight of the same book is the account of Philip and the Ethiopian. This man was an important official in charge of the finance department of Candace, Queen of the Ethiopians. After Philip had told him the good news of Jesus, he baptised him. Then we are told that the Spirit of the Lord suddenly took Philip away and he appeared at a place called Azotus many miles from where they had been. So the idea of being 'snatched away' from one place to another is not new in the Word of God.

But what happens after all the believers vanish without

warning off the face of the earth? Well, after this the news is not so good for those who are left behind, for after the Rapture a time of great dread will begin. This seven year period is called the Great Tribulation. This brief period is going to be so horrific that Jesus Christ said that unless those days are shortened, no flesh would be saved.

You may remember that when Jesus walked this earth, one of the statements he made was **'I am the light of the world. Whoever follows me will never walk in darkness, but will have the light of life'** (*John 8:12*). If you are walking in pitch darkness, and you have a light, then you can see where you are going. You can also see what is each side of you and what is behind you. If you come to a hole in the ground, you can walk around it. We are told that **God is Light** and that the world in which we live is in darkness and under the power of the 'Prince of Darkness'. But when we receive Jesus as Lord in our lives, then we get the gift of the Holy Spirit in us, and we become 'lights in this world'.

> **That you may be blameless and harmless, the sons of God without rebuke in the middle of a crooked and perverse world among whom ye shine as lights in this world.**
>
> *Philippians 2:15*

When Jesus walked this earth he could only be in one place at one time. Where he walked, the darkness had to go as he was 'the light'. Then after he ascended, the gift of the Holy Spirit was given at Pentecost. The apostles were filled with the same power as Jesus Christ had displayed when he walked. They preached the good news of the resurrection and demonstrated this truth by performing signs, miracles and wonders. Many thousands believed and got saved and began preaching and teaching themselves, converting many. In this way Christianity spread rapidly in the ensuing years. Every time a person believed, they got this free gift of holy spirit, which is eternal life. Then they became 'lights in this world'.

All the darkness in the world cannot put out the light. If you are in a darkened room and you switch on the light, the darkness has to go. When Satan crucified Jesus Christ, he thought he got rid of him forever. But Jesus was raised from death three days later and by doing so made the gift of the Holy Spirit available to anybody now who wishes to believe. So everywhere there is a Christian, there is a light. All over the globe there are many millions of lights. And all the time more lights are being added as people hear the word of God and decide to believe.

But when the Rapture happens, all the lights are going to disappear off this earth. Then all that is left will be darkness. This will make way for the devil to begin his short but bloody reign. The stage will be set for his representative, called the Antichrist, to make his appearance.

'Anti' means 'instead of' and not 'against' as most people think. So this man, who will be directly controlled by Satan, is 'instead of' Christ. He will be the devil's Messiah as it were. He will have a brief but eventful reign on the earth lasting seven years from the beginning of the Great Tribulation. This man will rise very fast on the world's political stage and gain tremendous power and influence. He will be the head of a confederacy of ten extremely rich and powerful 'kingdoms'. He will be the most charismatic and eloquent of all leaders. The world will love him. He will talk peace but will wage war. Most, but not all, will be deceived into thinking that he is the one who can bring peace to the world. How is this man going to gain such power? We can only speculate at this time. Historically many dictators rose to power on the back of some disaster or other in their homeland. Hitler, for instance, came to prominence after the economic collapse of Germany in the 1920s. So the Antichrist may well emerge as the man to lead the world in prosperity and peace, after some worldwide catastrophe. This could be a financial crash which looks more and more likely. Or perhaps a large scale military confrontation that almost pushes the world to the brink of nuclear holocaust. Or maybe his appearance will be as a result of the 'Rapture'. After all, there are an estimated 200 million real Christians in the world today. The confusion and financial chaos that will be caused as a result of their sudden removal could be catastrophic.

One way or another, this man will gain unprecedented worldwide political and military power. If we are close to the second coming of Christ, and I believe we are, then this man is being groomed for the job right now. If you are reading this and the Rapture has occurred, then watch out for the sudden rise of the greatest dictator of all time. Not only will he have wonderful presence and communication skills, but he will have apparently magical powers as well. With these he will deceive the whole world, except for the elect of God who will see through his mask. In *Apocalypse Soon* I proposed that this man will head up a confederacy of ten powerful European countries. Many of the experts in this field believe that the EU is the base for the ten nation confederacy which will be headed by this political leader. We shall return to this premise later.

This very powerful leader will have an ally. In *Revelation* this side-kick is called the 'False Prophet'. He will be a religious man who will give his support to the Antichrist. The 'False Prophet' will head up a worldwide religious movement which will look like the real thing, but it will be a sham. The 'False Prophet' will deceive many with 'lying signs and wonders'. He will have extraordinary spiritual powers which most people will believe come from God. But his source of power will be the devil himself.

In the first century the disciples of Christ did many 'signs, miracles and wonders' in the name of Jesus Christ. This man and his followers will do many signs miracles and wonders, but according to the Word of God, these will be 'lying signs and wonders'.

This new religious movement will have its basis in pagan worship, with an adherence to astrology and study of the signs of the Zodiac as its foundation. Again I believe we can already see the burgeoning of this future religious sect with the emergence of the New Age movement all over the world. But this is not 'new' because this religion is ancient with its foundations going back to Babylon in Old Testament times.

Sex will play a big part in the religious worship of the new doctrine. Also, the belief that we are all gods and all have the power within us to make peace with the planet and heal the planet, will be the main tenet on which this new religion is built.

We do not need an almighty God to pray to. Or a Jesus to come back to save us, for we can be at one with the spirit of the earth and we can save the planet by the power within us. Away with Jesus. Away with God the father, and away with people who believe in one God and Jesus. We must get rid of this cancer so that, at last we can begin the healing process and proceed to do what is necessary to make the world right. This is their *raison d'etre.*

Look around you. Already this country is filled with the disciples of New Age paganism. We see it everywhere and it is being propelled along by the media, especially television.

Constantly, we are being told to hearken back to our pre-Christian past. 'Celtic Spirituality' they call it – back to when the druids held sway.

I know of a New Age gathering in Carlow where, after copious amounts of alcohol and hash, the group ended in a wild orgy. The few women who were not paired off ended up rubbing themselves off the stones of the pagan ruin where they were worshipping. Likewise, a group of New Age friends from Galway went to a hill to practice their beliefs, where, after crawling around on all fours for a time to get in tune with the 'vibe' of the earth, one of them thought of having sex with the soil. 'So I did', one of them told me. He had intercourse with the actual ground!

Galway city is a microcosm of what is happening all over the country. It seems to have a large New Age pagan population.

Even the street festivals of Galway are redolent of a pagan era with evil-looking masks and fire-eating clowns and magicians all manifesting the New Age religion which is pervading this country.

This is similar to the situation in Sodom and Gomorrah prior to their destruction. *Ezekiel 16:49* provides some insight into the conditions which prevailed.

> **Behold, this was the iniquity of thy sister Sodom; pride, fullness of bread and abundance of idleness was in her and in her daughters.**

So here we are given three sins of Sodom:

1. **Pride**
2. **Fullness of Bread**
3. **Abundance of idleness**

This is an accurate description of many countries in the Western Hemisphere today. Because we are so well off, we do not need God. We are self-sufficient with fullness of bread and, as a result, abundance of idleness. It does not say here 'abundance of unemployment'. There is a difference. Many employers cannot get people to fill job vacancies in Ireland today yet there are still hundreds of thousands of people unemployed. This is because there is 'abundance of idleness' in the country.

These are the conditions that were prevalent in Sodom and Gomorrah before their destruction. These are the conditions Jesus told us to look for prior to His second coming.

A man walked by me in Dublin with a fashionable but revealing hairstyle – his head was shaven except for two little perfectly formed horns at the front of his head, just like a little devil. I saw an older man, perhaps in his thirties, with a little pointed beard, dyed bright green.

Both men and women are having their bodies pierced in various places now. This is the fashion. Most people regard this as just a phase, but to me it is the manifestation of this anti-

Christian paganism which will be the new world religion.

In Thomas Street in Dublin they have recently erected five statues that look as though they are fashioned from multi-coloured plasticine. They resemble five large ugly heads, similar to those discovered on the Easter Islands. We are told that this is art. But in reality they are manifestations of our pagan culture, for if we came across savages in the depths of the jungle, with their ear lobes pierced with huge rings, and bones through their noses, dancing around multi-coloured stautes of their gods, we would surely refer to them as pagans. Yet that is exactly what we have become, as witnessed by the multi-coloured totem pole erected in O'Connell Street.

In ancient times the sun and the penis were worhsipped as the givers of life. In many pagan countries, towers or obelisks or poles, representing the male organ, were erected pointing towards the sun in recognition of both their life-giving qualities. Egypt was a well-known centre for these phallic symbols. The obelisk that stands in St Peter's Square in Rome is the same obelisk that once stood at the ancient temple of Heliopolis which was the centre of Egyptian paganism. It was hauled to Rome at great expense by Caligula in 37-41 AD. So where these towers or obelisks are built, they represent the erect penis and act as a pagan symbol for the worship of sex.

And there is a proposal to have a 400 foot black metal spike erected where once Nelson's pillar stood in Dublin's O'Connell Street. This is a phallic pole to honour the god of our humanist, secular, material society, a monument to man's ego.

There is a spiritual void in this country and the religious are not filling it. Because of the recent scandals that have rocked the church, Roman Catholicism has lost its moral authority. Because we do not know the Bible and have little knowledge of the Word of God, good people are floundering in their faith. Because most priests have little knowledge or belief in the scriptures, they cannot feed their flocks. Empty religious rituals based on the traditions of men and the doctrines of men do not wash with the young people any more. So they fill the spiritual void with music, drugs, alcohol and sex. We have no legacy to give them.

This spiritual condition that we are witnessing all across the world is the genesis for the New Age religion which will have for its leader a man called in Revelation, the 'False Prophet'.

Together with the Antichrist, these two will bring the world into an era of pseudo peace. According to the prophet Daniel, this leader will sign a peace deal with Israel guaranteeing them military protection. The Jews will buy into this peace and the word of the Antichrist. But this era of peace and prosperity for the world will be short lived, for it will end with a war which will leave millions of Jews dead and the prospect of the one last great battle which will be fought over Jerusalem.

With the fall of the Berlin wall, and the dissipation of communism, the new buzz word is 'democracy'. All political leaders are working together to ensure peace and prosperity for all. World leaders and diplomats are constantly meeting in an effort to solve the problems of the world. The stage is being set for the revealing of a great political leader who will lead the world into a new era of peace. But this man will be the Antichrist, the son of the devil, and his goal will be total destruction. He cannot be revealed until after the believers are taken out. In the following passage, the Antichrist is called the *'the man of lawlessness'* and the *'lawless one'*.

> **Don't let anyone deceive you in any way, for that day will not come until the rebellion occurs and the man of lawlessness is revealed, the man doomed to destruction.**
> **He will oppose and will exalt himself over everything that is called God or is worshipped, so that he sets himself up in God's temple, proclaiming himself to be God.**
> **And now you know what is holding him back, so that he may be revealed at the proper time.**
> **For the secret power of lawlessness is already at work. But the one who now holds it back will continue to do so till he is taken out of the way.**
> **And then the lawless one will be revealed, whom the Lord Jesus**

will overthrow with the breath of his mouth and destroy by the splendour of His coming.
The coming of the lawless one will be in accordance with the work of Satan displayed in all kinds of counterfeit miracles, signs and wonders, and in every sort of evil that deceives those who are perishing. *II Thessalonians 2:3-4, 6-10*

Signs of the Times

IN THE FIRST AND second epistles of Paul to Timothy, we are given some more information as to the spiritual conditions of the 'last days' or 'latter days'. In the context, it is referring to the last days prior to the Rapture of the people of God and the subsequent beginning of the seven years of Great Tribulation. In the first Epistle to Timothy, Paul gives us an interesting insight:

> **The spirit clearly says that in the latter times some will abandon the faith and follow deceiving spirits and things taught by demons.** *1 Timothy 4:1*

I personally know people who at one time were practising Christians but who have now abandoned their faith. At one time these people were excited and thrilled at discovering the truths of the Word of God and the knowledge of Jesus Christ. But over the years their love waned and because of temptations, they have forsaken the truth and turned to beliefs taught by demons.

The above verse tells us these people are tricked by deceiving spirits and demons. Deception is a subtle thing and leads to another sign of the last days – apostasy.

This is a turning away from God and from Christian morals, and a reliance on self. For hundreds of years the

Western Hemisphere has prospered because it has relied on Christian principles and the laws originally given to Moses. But now many of these laws are being abandoned and turned on their head. On an almost universal scale we can see that man is living totally opposite to the precepts of Christian principles.

> **But mark this: there will be terrible times in the last days. People will be lovers of themselves, lovers of money, boastful, proud, abusive, disobedient to their parents, ungrateful, unholy, without love, unforgiving, slanderous, without self control, brutal, not lovers of the good, treacherous, rash, conceited lovers of pleasure rather than lovers of God.** *2 Timothy 3:1-5*

The Christian ideal is the totally opposite to all of the above. But when we look around us at society today, what we witness is exactly what is stated in the above passage. Today, people *love themselves*. We are told in the second commandment that we should love our neighbour as ourselves. But people today love themselves in a selfish, egotistical manner. As a result they are proud and boastful.

Lovers of money – was there ever a time in history where money was so important? Today for most people money is God. Unless people have it, they cannot be content. Our whole life seems to revolve around the pursuit of money. And once we have it, we become lovers of pleasure rather than lovers of God. And people who acquire money usually become proud. In fact, pride is the one sin we can readily see in other people but never in ourselves. And pride always comes before a fall.

In the last days, people will become *'abusive, disobedient to their parents, ungrateful, unholy'*. We are becoming more and more insular. And people are 'ungrateful'. We take things for granted and very seldom pause to say thanks, for we have become 'unholy'. We have no regard for the 'higher powers'. Society is getting more and more materialistic and less and less spiritual.

In the last days, Paul says people will be *'without love'*

meaning they will become more callous and hardened. Jesus said the same when speaking of the last days. **'Because lawlessness will increase, the love of many will grow cold'** (*Matthew 24:12*). Thus they become 'unforgiving' for their hearts turn to stone because of their propensity for sin. People will become *'slanderous'*. This means they are liars. This is especially evident in some political leaders today. In this country we have political people who are liars and lovers of money. They are even arrogant when caught which demonstrates their pride. And when they get a chance to remonstrate, they proceed to boast about all the 'good' they did for the country.

Not 'lovers of the good' means they will hate and despise those who believe in Jesus Christ and try to promote Christian morals and teachings. In the last days people will be 'Lovers of pleasure rather that lovers of God'. Party, party, party. If it feels good, just do it. All over the world, getting stoned and having sex is what is fashionable – from Bali to Belmullet, from Rio to Roscommon.

If ever a time in history was in keeping with Paul's description of the spiritual conditions of the last days, it is now. But if we are aware of these things then we do not need to be deceived by them.

> **The day of the Lord will come like a thief in the night.**
> **While people are saying, 'Peace and Safety', destruction will come on them suddenly, as labour pains on a pregnant woman, and they will not escape.**
> **But you, brothers, are not in darkness so that this day should surprise you like a thief.**
> **You are all sons of the light and sons of the day. We do not belong to night or to darkness.** *1 Thessalonians 5:2-5*

We are never told by God or Jesus that the world will get better before He comes back. We are told, however, that things will get progressively worse. Wars and rumours of wars ... famines and earthquakes, unusual weather, increase in violence, child pornography, teenage pregnancies, abortion on demand, rampant child abuse, corruption in high places, low morals in the clergy ... the list is endless.

Violence and murder is almost a daily occurrence in Ireland today. What is the world coming to? All these are indications that we are living in the generation that will witness the return of Jesus Christ. And this is our one and only hope, for without the certainty of His second coming, we are doomed. But the good news is that he is coming back to rescue us from the wrath to come. After the wrath he will begin to put this old world back in order. This is our certain hope.

Revelation Unveiled

> **The revelation of Jesus Christ, which God gave to him to show his servants what must soon take place.**
>
> *The Book of Revelation 1:1*

SOME PEOPLE CALL THIS book *'The Revelation of St John the Divine'*. But this is wrong. Its divine title is **'The Revelation of Jesus Christ'**. The Greek word for revelation is *Apokalupsis* which means unveiling. Thus Jesus Christ is unveiling the course of future events in the same way as you would draw curtains back so we can view a stage. It can also mean the taking away of the veil so that we can see the face. In this book both senses are true, for Jesus Christ is unveiling the events so that we may see what lies ahead. Also, in this future time, all will see the face of Jesus Christ. *The Book of Revelation* has for centuries been a closed book. Even students of the Bible have very little understanding of it. Much of the events regarding the last days of this world as we know it are stated in this book. Other prophetic passages from both the Old and New Testaments come to fruition in this book. The prophet Daniel received much information regarding these end days. When he had recorded it, God told him to **'seal up the words of this prophecy until the time of the end'**. It is for this reason I believe few have been able to decipher its secrets.

But now *The Book of Revelation* is beginning to unveil. And, although it contains descriptions of chaos and holocaust, we are assured by Jesus Christ himself that we are blessed if we read or hear these words.

> **Blessed is the one who reads the words of this prophecy, and blessed are those who hear it, and who take to heart what is written in it, because the time is near.** *Revelation 1:3*

Many ministers and religious teachers spend much of their time and energy teaching and preaching the writings of the gospels and epistles and yet ignore *The Book of Revelation.* This is a paradox for in this last book of the Bible we have Jesus himself speaking directly to us, for it is His revelation.

In this section, I will endeavour to give a summary of some of the events prophesied in *Revelation.* This is no easy job as it is quite hard to decode and even harder to make plain a lot of it. As I said before, *Revelation* is a conundrum wrapped in an enigma and surrounded by a paradox. However, I shall do my utmost to explain the parts that are understandable and tie these in with other parallel prophecies from scripture.

Off the south-eastern coast of Turkey lies a small island named Patmos. The apostle John was incarcerated on this island because of his preaching of the resurrection of Jesus Christ. The Romans had a quarry on this spot and John probably worked out his sentence here. He was an old man in his nineties at this stage. It was while he was here that he received the revelation and was instructed to write down what he saw and heard. Then we read in verse one of chapter four:

> **After this I looked and there before me was a door standing open in heaven. And the voice I had first heard like a trumpet said 'Come up here and I will show you what must take place after this'.**

He then goes on to describe what he saw in this other place called 'heaven'. What he describes is an amazing spectacle. He sees a throne and the one who is sitting on this throne is God. This throne is surrounded by 24 other thrones who we are told, are occupied by 24 elders. Who these elders are, we do not know. But they bow down and worship God.

After this, John tells us, he sees in the right hand of him who sits on the throne, a scroll with writing on both sides and sealed with Seven Seals. But who is worthy to open these seals and look inside? John weeps because no one in heaven or on earth was found who could open the seals and look inside.

Then he sees a lamb standing in the midst of the throne. He came and took the scroll from the right hand of him who sat on the throne. Then all the elders sing:

> **You are worthy to take the scroll and open its seals.**
> **Because you were slain and with your blood you purchased men for God.** *Revelation 5:9*

Then the throne was encircled by 10,000 times 10,000 angels, (which is 100 million of these spirit men) and they began singing and praising the one who sat on the throne and the Lamb, who is Jesus.

In chapter six, John watched as the lamb opened the first of the seven seals:

> **I looked and there before me was a white horse. Its rider held a bow, and he was given a crown, and he rode out as a conqueror bent on conquest.**
> **The lamb opened the second seal. Then another horse came out, a fiery red one. Its rider was given power to take peace from the earth and make men slay each other. To him was given a large sword.**
> **The lamb opened the third seal: and there before me was a black horse. Its rider was holding a pair of scales in his hand.**
> **Then I heard what sounded like a voice saying 'A quart of wheat for a days wages, and three quarts of barley for a days wages, and do not damage the oil and the wine'.**
> **The lamb opened the fourth seal: I looked, and there before me was a pale horse. Its rider was named death, and Hades was following close behind him. They were given power over a fourth**

> **of the earth to kill by sword, famine and plague, and by the wild beasts of the earth.** *Revelation 6:1-8*

These are sometimes referred to as the Four Horsemen of the Apocalypse. But what does it all mean? To find out, we go back to the parallel passage in *Matthew Chapter 24.*

The first thing we are told to watch out for according to Jesus is false prophets and false Christs. Many will go out to deceive many, he said. He also told us to watch out for the one great false deceiver who would say **'I am the Messiah'** (*Matthew 24:5*). This is the Antichrist who will emerge on the world political stage soon after the Rapture. He will put himself forward as the one who can bring peace to a world on the brink of war and turmoil.

The people of the world will welcome this man with open arms. They will believe they need to unite under a strong dictator who can deliver peace. This is why we see the first rider appear on a white horse with a bow with no arrow, for he will promise peace and reconciliation. It will be he who will broker a peace deal between Israel and the Arab nations guaranteeing them protection. This will mark the beginning of the seven years of Tribulation according to the prophet Daniel *(Daniel 7:27*). This will lead to a spurious period of stability and peace. Even the Jews will trust this powerful political leader. But although everyone will love this man and believe they are entering a new era of world peace, his tenure will end in the greatest military holocaust ever witnessed on the earth.

So the rider on the white horse is the Counterfeit Christ, also called the man of sin, son of perdition, the Antichrist.

If we are close to the fulfillment of these days, and I believe we are, then this man will already be in position. Right now he is being groomed for the job by Satan, for he will be working for and in direct communication with the devil.

We can see from the way things are developing in the world politically that the stage is being set for one world government.

Who would have thought just a few short years ago, that the cold war would be over? Who could have envisaged the total collapse of communism in Russia and eastern Europe in such a short time? Almost overnight the world's political landscape changed. Now the buzz word is democracy. It is sweeping the world with the promise of freedom and prosperity for all. People are being encouraged to work together to ensure a stable future for everyone. Democracy is the vehicle and money is the oil that promises to deliver this better future for all mankind. This will be the promise of the rider on the white horse.

> **Then another horse came out, a fiery red one. Its rider was given power to take peace from the earth and make men slay each other. To him was given a large sword.**

The second sign Jesus spoke of in *Matthew 24* was '**ye shall hear of wars and rumours of wars ... nation shall rise against nation, and kingdom against kingdom**'. This relates directly to the rider on the red horse, for in the Great Tribulation, after a pseudo peace which will last a relatively short time, all hell will break loose. All the places around the world that are in a stand off situation at the moment, will erupt in conflict. The potential for war is massive. In almost every country in the world there is the possibility of huge bloodshed.

The world at the present time is at a dangerous crossroads with hundreds of conflicts going on and hundreds more just bubbling under the surface, waiting to erupt. When the rider on the fiery red horse is let loose, all these tensions will be realised with war and slaughter on a scale that no one could even imagine.

> **The lamb opened the third seal: and there before me was a black horse. Its rider was holding a pair of scales in his hand.**
> **Then I heard what sounded like a voice saying:**
> **'A quart of wheat for a days wages, and three quarts of barley for a days wages, and do not damage the oil and the wine'.**

Again we relate this to the third sign given by Jesus Christ when he foretold of those last days: **there will be famines**. The rider on the black horse delivers these famines. Black always denotes famine. And weighing out of bread always denotes scarcity. There have been many famines foretold before in the Bible. Take the story of Joseph and his multi-coloured coat. When the Pharoah had a dream, he could not find anyone in his court who could interpret the dream for him. He tried all his soothsayers, mediums, fortune tellers and astrologers. But they were void of useful information in those days, just as they are void of the truth in our day.

So Pharoah called for Joseph. He asked Joseph if he could interpret the dream. Joseph replied that he could not, but that God would give him the answer. The Pharoah told Joseph his dream. He was standing on the bank of the Nile. Seven fat healthy cows came up out of the river. Then these were followed by seven lean skinny ugly cows who swallowed up the fat, healthy cows.

Then he saw seven ears of corn, healthy and good and growing on a single stalk. After them came seven other ears of corn, thin and scorched by the east wind. The seven thin ears swallowed up the seven healthy, full ears.

Joseph told him that the two dreams were the same. Egypt was going to experience seven years of great abundance of food and crops. But these would be followed by seven years of famine. This famine would ravage the land and the seven years of abundance would be forgotten because the famine would be so severe.

He suggested to Pharoah that he choose a man to oversee the economy for the seven good years. This man would build warehouses and store one-fifth of the harvest during the seven years of plenty so that they would have enough food to sustain them through the seven years of famine.

Pharoah listened to the interpretation and knew it made sense. He also knew that if he followed Joseph's advice it would make total sense. So he gave Joseph the job. He elevated him so that only Pharoah was above Joseph in the whole Egyptian empire. From being the lowest of the low in the state jail, Joseph was elevated to the highest office in the land. And all because he trusted in his God.

Later in the story we find that everything happened just as Joseph said it would. After the seven years of abundance there followed seven years of bitter famine. During this time all the countries around about came to Egypt to buy food to sustain them through the famine. In this short seven years, Egypt amassed all the gold and treasure of these nations by selling them food. This is historical fact.

Now the rider on the black horse denotes a coming famine. You can scoff at this prospect or you can believe it. Pharoah was wise enough to take to heart the prophesy and to do something about it.

I believe this black rider is foretelling of a great economic holocaust. For a day's wages is a mere quart of wheat and three quarts of barley. One way or another this is describing the collapse of the economic and monetary systems of the world. All around us today we get signs of this impending financial collapse. Much of the welfare of the system is based on confidence. It would not take much to send the financial markets into free-fall.

There are some likely situations which could precipitate just such a financial crash. For instance, many experts believe that the failure of computers to register the year 2000 could cause mayhem all over the globe. Despite repeated warnings, many computers are still not year 2000 compliant. This could cause a world-wide economic catastrophe.

Either way, the world will experience a global famine and economic collapse. I believe we are already seeing signs of a possible collapse world-wide on our televisions and by watching the business pages in our newspapers.

Even if the Rapture of Christians does not happen soon, the

possibilities of a crash and subsequent food shortages seems extremely likely.

Indeed, most of the vegetables we now eat come from Holland or Cyprus or Spain or elsewhere. To be forewarned is to be forearmed. If you take my advice, what have you got to lose? Or on the other hand, if I am right and these predictions do come upon us soon, we need to be prepared.

The black horse and his rider warn us of the famine that will ravish the earth. You do not have to go through this awful time if you heed my words. Put your trust in God and in His son Jesus Christ. Anyone who calls on His name will be saved.

> **The lamb opened the fourth seal: I looked and there before me was a pale horse. Its rider was named death, and Hades followed close behind him.**
> **They were given power over a fourth of the earth to kill by sword, famine and plague, and by the wild beasts of the earth.**
> *Revelation 6:8*

This is the fourth judgement mentioned by Jesus in *Matthew 24:7* '**Pestilences**'. Though the Greek word used here is *Thanatos* meaning death, it is put by a Metonymy, as the effect for the cause producing it, which is pestilence or diseases. (A Metonymy is a substitution of one word for another when the objects each refers to are habitually associated). 'Pestilence' is followed by the grave (Hades) and the two words occur together because the latter depends on the former. Hades follows in the train of Death, because Death ends in the grave. Wars, famines and the resulting pestilence are the agencies used by death and are always followed by a common result – the grave.

Hades is the place which holds the dead, but Jesus, we are told, holds the keys to Hades. It is He who raises the dead and it is via Him we can escape the grave.

We discussed earlier the huge problem at present with the spread of pestilence or disease.

Yet what we are seeing now is nothing compared to the

devastation that will be unleashed in the Great Tribulation, for we are told that when you add up the figures provided in *Revelation* you arrive at a terrible conclusion. We are told that half the population of the world will die as a result of the wars, famines and diseases that these horsemen represent. At today's figures this means approximately three billion people will die.

Again we are urged to heed the words of Jesus when he said:

> **When you see all these things begin to come to pass, lift up your heads. Your redemption is near.**

Is it not patently obvious that these prophecies, written almost 2,000 years ago, are unfolding before our very eyes? We were told that these events would be like a woman in labour pains. The contractions become more frequent and more violent as the actual birth draws closer. So too you will see all these things become more frequent and more violent as we approach the final convulsion that will be the seven years of Great Tribulation.

When a woman goes into the final throes of labour, they describe it as panic, fear, out of control and no going back. Thus this world must inevitably go through the anxiety, pain and blood of the Great Tribulation before it can be reborn into the freedom of Paradise regained.

> **I tell you the truth, until heaven and earth disappear, not the smallest letter, nor the least stroke of a pen, will by any means disappear from the law until everything is accomplished.**
>
> *Jesus Christ - Matthew 5:18*

The Seven Seals, Seven Trumpets, Seven Vials

THE FIFTH, SIXTH AND seventh seals are then opened. I will give a brief summation:

The Fifth Seal

After the Rapture or *'catching away'* of the Christians, there will still be a huge population left behind to go through the seven years of wrath. Many people who scoff at us Christians now and who mock and refuse to listen or accept our warnings, will be isolated. People will turn to God and to Jesus Christ for salvation and help. It is going to be a hard seven years but there is hope.

We are told that a large amount of Jews will be converted to Christ in this Tribulation. These will number 144,000 in all, 12,000 from each of the twelve tribes of Israel. Somehow, these 144,000 are converted and become vigorous and powerful evangelists. As a result of their preaching, multitudes of people are going to believe and realise that Jesus Christ is their only hope. But there is a down-side here, for many of these believers will die as a result of their faith.

We are told later on that the Antichrist will demand

absolute allegiance. This will mean that everyone must take a mark or brand in their right hand or on their forehead. This mark is a number. It is the mark of the Beast and his number is 666. Anyone who refuses to take this mark cannot buy or sell or do business. And many who refuse because of their faith will be executed by the Antichrist and his one world government forces. The inference from the fifth seal is that large numbers of Christians will die during the Tribulation period.

The Sixth Seal

This talks of a huge earthquake that is so massive every mountain and every island is removed out of its place. People of the world are so terrified, they call on the rocks to fall on them:

> **Fall on us, and hide us from the face of him who sits on the throne and from the wrath of the lamb.**
> **For the great day of their wrath has come, and who can stand?**
> *Revelation 6:16,17*

The Seventh Seal

The Seventh Seal introduces the seven trumpet judgements. These are another series of woes that fall upon the earth in due course. After these trumpet judgements, there are another series of judgements called the vial judgements. There are seven of these also.

We do not know if all these judgements occur at the same time or are consecutive to one another. However, we will submit a brief summary of these trumpet and vial judgements. Later we will focus on particular elements of these.

First Trumpet: *Revelation 8:7*

When the first angel sounds his trumpet, hail and fire mixed with blood is cast down upon the earth. One-third of all the grass and one-third of all the trees are burned up.

First Vial: *Revelation 16:2*

The first vial is poured out and causes horrible sores to appear on those who have the mark of the Beast. We learned that one-third of all grass and all trees and plants would be burnt up at the first trumpet. Could it be that what we are seeing develop right now with the Ozone layer could be a precursor to these woes? Already in many countries people are being scorched by the sun because of damage done to the ozone layer.

Scientists are saying that if the depletion of the ozone reaches 15%, millions will die from skin cancer. In southern Chile, people are already being burned and animals blinded by the harmful rays of the sun. This is caused by the release of harmful CFCs which deplete the thin ozone layer and allow destructive rays from the sun to enter the atmosphere without being filtered. Once the thin ozone layer is destroyed, it cannot be repaired. The effect of this will be an increase in world temperatures and global warming. As a result we can expect to see the world food supply decrease, with an increase in famines as a result.

All these environmental hazards fit in exactly with the prophecies of the end times. And this is not just my opinion. These are scientific facts.

Second Trumpet: *Revelation 8:8,9*
When this second trumpet is sounded something looking like a huge mountain all ablaze is thrown into the sea. As a result all life in one-third of the oceans die and one-third of all ships are destroyed.

Second Vial: *Revelation 16:3*
The second vial is similar to that of the second trumpet when a huge burning object, resembling a star, will fall into the sea and destroy all life and all ships in one-third of the seas.

This could be a meteor. Or there again John could be describing some type of nuclear holocaust. It could be another environmental disaster like that of Chernobyl. What would be the consequences if an earthquake were to erupt underneath the

Selafield nuclear plant? Jesus told us in his discourse on the Mount of Olives that there would be an increase in earthquakes and volcanoes in the last days. Already this is happening with earthquakes becoming an almost weekly occurrence. However, those living in the last seven years can expect to see one-third of the sea die and one-third of all marine vessels destroyed when this 'burning star' hits the oceans.

Third Trumpet: *Revelation 8:10,11*
This announces a huge star or meteor called 'Wormwood'. It falls like a blazing torch onto all the fresh water rivers and springs of water. This pollutes these waters in one-third of all the world and many die as a result of drinking the poisoned water.

Third Vial: *Revelation 16:4*
The third vial causes the springs and fountains of drinking water to be turned into 'blood'. This fits in with the third trumpet which John described as another huge star blazing like a torch, which fell upon the fresh springs and polluted one-third of all water. Anybody who drinks this water will die. The name of the star is 'Wormwood'.

How many countries in the world have biological weapons of war? A great many, I would suggest. We know these deadly weapons are already on the market. A small amount of one such poison, poured into a reservoir, could kill two million people. And there are radical fundamentalist Muslims who would love to inflict this form of 'justice' on the West, particularly America, whom they hate.

Whether this Wormwood is germ warfare or another nuclear fallout, we shall have to wait to see. But the potential for either is a stark reality in our precarious and fickle world.

Fourth Trumpet: *Revelation 8:12*
As a result of this trumpet, one-third of all light disappears. The

sun, moon and stars lose one-third of their light. This will have catastrophic results on the temperature of the earth.

Fourth Vial: *Revelation 16: 8, 9*

> **The fourth angel poured out this bowl on the sun, and the sun was given power to scorch people with fire.**
> **They were seared by the intense heat and they cursed the name of God, who had control over these plagues, but they refused to repent and glorify him.** *Revelation: 6: 8, 9*

Fifth Trumpet: *Revelation 9:1 -12*
As if things were not bad enough we have an eagle flying in mid-air proclaiming in a loud voice:

> **Woe, woe, woe to the inhabitants of the earth because of the trumpet blasts about to be sounded by the other three angels.**
> *Revelation 8:13*

This fifth trumpet introduces an evil scenario. We are told that a place called the Abyss is unlocked. Out of this pit come hideous demon-like creatures that look like locusts. These creatures have the power to torture with their sting but not to kill.

They cannot touch those who are 'sealed' by God however. These are protected. But everyone else is prey to these scorpion-like demons who can torture for five months. Because of this agony, men will seek death, but will not find it. They will long to die, but death will elude them.

Fifth Vial: *Revelation 16: 10, 11*
When the fifth vial is poured out there will be darkness over the 'kingdom' of the 'Beast'.

> **Men gnawed their tongues in agony and cursed the God of heaven because of their pains and their sores, but they refused to repent of what they had done.** *Revelation 16: 10, 11*

Sixth Trumpet: *Revelation 9:13*
The angel that blows the sixth trumpet releases mounted troops numbering 200 million. These 200 million troops kill one-third of mankind as they sweep across the breadth of the earth. Going on today's figures, they will slay *circa* two billion people.

Sixth Vial: *Revelation 16: 12*
The sixth vial is poured out on the river Euphrates causing it to 'dry up' and allow the 'kings of the East' to march unhindered towards the Middle East and the final showdown beginning at Armageddon. This fits in with the sixth trumpet which described an army numbering 200 million who would come from the East and slaughter one-third of the world's population on their westward march.

The Euphrates has always been the ancient dividing line between the Middle East and the Orient. In the original Greek, *east* is literally translated as 'king of the sun rising'. This is an obvious reference to the people of Asia. This prophecy says an army numbering 200 million will cross the Euphrates to engage with troops from the West. China is the only country that can today muster an army of 200 million. Yet this prophecy was penned almost 2,000 ago. How the jigsaw is fitting together!

There now go out 'deceiving' spirits and they motivate the 'kings of the earth' to gather in preparation for battle. The sixth vial ends having gathered all the hosts of the enemy thither to battle.

The Seventh Trumpet: *Revelation 11:15*
This introduces the vial judgements which take place in chapters 12-18. These events are more terrible than the ones already experienced: Although we are given these seals, trumpets and vial judgements in order, there is a lot of evidence that they are all happening at the same time, for all these judgements end up in the seventh judgement which is common to all three: a huge earthquake.

> **Then I heard a loud voice from the temple saying to the seven angels, 'Go, pour out the seven bowls of God's wrath on the earth'.** *Revelation 16:1*

Seventh Vial: *Revelation 16: 18*
The pouring out of the seventh vial coincides with the seventh seal and seventh trumpet. This describes a catastrophic earthquake that will destroy cities and cause islands to disappear. This earthquake will be followed by hail stones from the sky which will weigh around 100 pounds each and will fall on men. But in each of the three final judgements it says the earthquake is preceded by:

> **... Flashes of lightning, rumblings, peals of thunder and a severe earthquake.** *Revelations:15: 18*

We cannot know for sure exactly what this can mean. But looking back on recent history and looking forward at the scenario that is unfolding, this sounds like an all-out nuclear strike. As has been pointed out previously, Jesus said that if *'Those days had not been cut short, no one would survive' (Matthew 24: 22).* Man today possesses the weaponry to wipe out all life on planet earth seven times over. The powers of the world are gearing up for this day. Although the Valley of Megiddo is the focal point, all the world will be involved in this conflagration.

The reason it will begin in this area is because this is the centre of the world biblically. Jerusalem is the most important city spiritually. The word *Mediterranean* means 'middle of the world'. World peace is contingent upon what happens in Israel. The whole Arab/Israeli conflict is what will draw all these vast armies to this region. And the *raison d'etre* for them being there is the huge oil reserves of the Middle East. There is much prophecy about Jerusalem in these final days and how it will be a rock on which many nations will perish. We are told that the fighting in this area will be so fierce that the blood will reach up to the bridles of the horses to a distance of 200 miles away.

Who would have thought that a small nation of around five million people occupying such a tiny area could be the fuse that blows up the world? Yet just as all the other prophecies that have been thus far fulfilled, so too will be the gathering of the armies of the world to the valley called Armageddon. But the good news is you don't have to be around to see it.

The Abyss

AFTER THE FIFTH ANGEL sounds his trumpet in *Revelation 9,* we are confronted with a frightening picture. A 'star' is given the key to the abyss. Usually a star is another name for an angel of God. He is the jailer to the abyss. Out of this abyss comes smoke and out of the smoke locusts that have the power to torture but not to kill. They can sting everybody except those who have the seal of God on their foreheads. But this sting does not kill only tortures people who receive it for five months.

> **And the agony they suffered was like that of the sting of the scorpion when it strikes a man.**
> **During those days men will seek death, but will to not find it; they will long to die, but death will elude them.**
>
> *Revelation 9:5,6*

The abyss crops up a few times in scripture. You remember the man who was possessed by the legion of demons. The demons begged Jesus not to cast them into the abyss. Also we learn in 1 *Peter 3:19,* that Jesus in his new, resurrected body went and displayed himself to the spirits who were imprisoned in the abyss. These evil spirits, we are told, are the same fallen angels who were responsible for the wickedness that prevailed in the world prior to the flood in Noah's day. These fallen angels left their own estate and had sexual intercourse with ordinary women thus producing a kind of giant demonic race of people who were exceedingly evil. Goliath was one of these giants. We do not know nor are we told how this could be, but we know it happened.

For their wickedness and evil, the demons responsible for the events of that time are held in prison in this place called the abyss or 'bottomless pit'. How can evil spirits have sex with women? I do not know. But these evil spirits who come out of the Abyss are real, actual demons. And when they are released in the Great Tribulation, they will wreak havoc on the unbelieving people of the world. We are told also in this chapter 9 of a huge army from the East who number 200 million strong. This army, we are told, will slaughter one-third of the world's population as it cuts its way westward towards the Middle East. That means in today's terms that up to two billion people will be massacred by this army. John was shown a vision almost 2,000 years ago and he had to describe what he saw in terms of his own experience. Could it be that what he is describing is in fact a twentieth-century high-tech war?

> **And this is how I saw in the vision the horses and those that sat on them: The riders had breastplates the colour of fire and dark blue and of yellow as sulphur. The heads of the horses are like the heads of lions and out of their mouths came smoke, fire and sulphur.**
> **A third of mankind was killed by these three plagues, by the fire and the smoke and the brimstone that came out of their mouths. For the power of the horses is in their mouths and in their tails: for their tails were like snakes, having heads with which they inflict injury.** *Revelation 9:17-19*

Is John describing real creatures or is he describing a nuclear war? It sounds like modern warfare when he speaks of smoke, fire and sulphur. Perhaps he is describing firing missiles, for these weapons kill one-third of mankind in a very short space of time. He talks of horses and those that ride on them. He says their power was in their head and in their tails. This has to be missiles which explode when their head hits its target. The tails he says, were like snakes. This is the trail a missile leaves behind as it snakes through the air en route to its victim. This applies to the earlier description of the locusts from the abyss.

> **The locusts look like horses prepared for battle. On their heads they wore something like crowns of gold, and their faces resembled human faces.**
> **Their hair was like a woman's hair, and their teeth were like lions' teeth.**
> **They had breastplates like breastplates of iron, and the sound of their wings was like the thundering of many horses and chariots rushing into battle.**
> **They had tails and stings like scorpions and in their tails they had power to torment people for five months.** *Revelation 9:7-10*

When John talks of a head with a crown and a human face, could he be describing the headgear of a helicopter pilot? When a helicoptor rotates its blades it resembles a woman's hair blowing in the breeze. And the noise from them would resemble many horses and chariots going to war. The stings in their tails could be their guns and missiles and the sting they produce could be the effect of germ warfare. He said these locusts had wings which sounded like the thundering of many horses rushing into battle. Well, locusts fly and swarm in great numbers. John has to be describing the war planes and bombers and helicopters that resemble locusts when hundreds of them are attacking. I believe he called them locusts because he is seeing a vision of something in the future which is totally alien to him. Remember, John was in his nineties when he saw this vision. So when he sees a swarm of aircraft flying, he can only describe them in terms of his own experience. He said they had teeth like lions' teeth. The missiles and rockets that fighter aircraft and helicoptors carry look like lions' teeth.

He had never experienced the roar from their engines so he says they sound like the thundering of many horses and chariots rushing into battle. What John is trying to describe is a huge aerial assault using the latest high-tech weapons by a vast amount of fighter aircraft.

Perhaps these evil spirits that are released are the invisible forces that are behind and motivate the high-tech warfare that will culminate at the second half of the seven years of the Great Tribulation. So, too, perhaps these descriptions are John trying to put into words a high-tech nuclear clash of the last days, for Jesus said 'except those days be shortened, no flesh should be saved' (*Matthew 24:22*). In the world today we have weapons and fire power capable of wiping out all life on the earth several times over. When you add up the figures given in *Revelation*, we are told that half the population of the world will die in this future holocaust. In today's terms that would be almost three billion people. Should we therefore be afraid? No.

Almost everybody realises that the world is on a slippery slope. They can all see the dangers ahead, but only Christians have the answer. The people who should be afraid are those who stick their heads in the sand and say 'everything is going to be alright'. We should pray for them and try to get them to examine the proof of prophecy. Then perhaps, they may have a chance of avoiding the chaos of the last days.

Two Witnesses

IN CHAPTER 11 WE are given an account of the 'Two Witnesses'. These two men God will raise up and empower. Nobody knows who these men will be. Some believe one will be Elijah who was taken up and Raptured in the Old Testament (see *II Kings* 2). In the days of Ahab, Elijah shut up heaven so that no rain fell for three and a half years (*I Kings 17.1*). This is exactly what it says in *Revelation* regarding God's two witnesses.

> **If anyone tries to harm them, fire comes from their mouths and devours their enemies.**
>
> **These men have the power to shut up the sky so that it will not rain during the time they are prophesying. And they have the power to turn the waters into blood and to strike the earth with every kind of plague as often as they want.**
>
> *Revelation 11:5-6*

The second witness, some believe, will be Moses for only he had the power to turn water into blood and cause plagues to come on the land as he did when in captivity in Egypt (*Exodus 7:19, 19:15*). Also, on the Mount of Transfiguration, it was Moses and Elijah who appeared and spoke to Jesus *(Matthew 17:1-11)*. All the powers that these two men are empowered with were already exercised by Moses and Elijah in Old Testament times.

But we are not specifically told who these two are in this future time so we may only speculate. These two witnesses will prophesy against the powers that be for three and a half years. The Antichrist and his minions will hate them exceedingly but are powerless to kill them until the three and a half years are finished. Then the *'beast from the abyss'* will attack them and kill them. Their two slain bodies are left on the streets for three and a half days. We are told that the people of the earth will gaze on their corpses and rejoice in their deaths because these two prophets had tormented them for so long. They send one another gifts and delight in their murder. But then something amazing happens.

> **But after the three and a half days the breath of life from God entered them and they stood on their feet, and terror struck those who saw them.**
> **And they went up to heaven in a cloud while their enemies looked on.** *Revelation 11:11,12*

The only way the people of the nations could have viewed this scene is on global television, for we are told that the earth will see their dead bodies in the street. Of course, this does not sound surprising until you realise it was penned almost 2,000 years ago. The unbelievers are having a party to celebrate the death of these two 'fundamentalists' when suddenly they come back to life and stand up. As the people who watch are seized by fear, the two prophets are taken up to heaven in a cloud just as Jesus was in *Acts 1:10,11*. Of course many believe these predictions to be but mere flights of fancy, that no such thing will ever happen. Let me tell you, the whole Bible is full of miracles and almost unbelievable feats. From the dividing of the Red Sea to Jesus feeding the 5,000 with a few loaves and fishes. From God creating the universe to Jesus raising Lazarus from the dead. The whole Book is a book of signs, miracles and wonders.

Even *The Book of Revelation* is a phenomenal miracle. For

right now you are reading history before it happens. And you can rest assured, all these things will happen. Some day the people of the world will experience these two prophets who will witness for God. And that day may be closer than we think.

Cosmic Battle

CHAPTER 12 OF *REVELATION* describes a battle in heaven between Satan and his evil angels on the one hand and Michael and his angels on the other. Apparently, Satan still has access to the heavenly realm, for we are told in *Job 1:6-12*, that Satan entered the presence of God. And in this chapter it says the same.

> **For the accuser of our brothers, who accuses them before our God day and night, has been hurled down.** *Revelation 12:10*

However, a battle ensues and Satan is defeated and cast down to earth and his angels with him.

> **And there was war in heaven. Michael and his angels fought against the dragon and his angels. But he was not strong enough, and they lost their place in heaven.**
> **The great dragon was hurled down – that ancient serpent called the devil, or Satan, who leads the whole world astray.**
> **He was hurled to the earth and his angels with him.**
> *Revelation 12:7-9*

When the devil is cast out of heaven, he is filled with wrath, for he knows his time is short. So he goes after what is called 'the woman' to kill her. This is a figure of speech referring to Israel. The devil now tries to kill all the remaining Jews. But God helps them to flee into the desert where they are protected for three and a half years. The devil then goes after those Christians who obey God's word.

It is during the second half of the seven years of Tribulation that all hell, literally, is going to break out. For the devil, having been expelled from heaven, knows that he has but a short time left. It is interesting that in the above verse he is referred to as 'he who leads the whole world astray'.

We are left in no doubt as to who this is for he is given five titles here: 'the **dragon**, the old **serpent**, the **devil** or **Satan**: the **accuser**'. Jesus referred to this future expulsion when he made a prophetic statement in *The Gospel of Luke*:

> **I saw Satan fall like lightning from heaven.** *Luke 10:18*

It is after Satan is driven out of heaven and down to earth that he completely takes control of his chosen one, the Antichrist, and this man literally becomes the devil incarnate. Now he will break the peace treaty he earlier made with the Jews and will seek to destroy them. He will also at this time determine to exterminate all who have turned to Jesus Christ and refuse to accept the mark of the Beast. Many Christians will be martyred for their faith during this harsh time.

The Brand of Hell

TWO BEASTS ARE FEATURED in chapter 13. The first beast is the Antichrist who we know will be a political leader. He will appear on the world stage after the Rapture of the church. We are told in this chapter, that the first beast, the Antichrist, appears to receive a deadly head wound which is fatal. But miraculously, he is healed of this fatal wound and lives again. We can only surmise as to the details of this miracle. Perhaps this political leader is assassinated. Everybody knows he is dead but then he is raised from the dead by the power of the dragon (Satan) and as a result, the whole world worships him and worships the dragon who gave the Antichrist his authority.

As we said before, the word *'anti'* does not mean *'against'* but *'instead of'*. He will be instead of 'Christ', and the world will embrace him just as it rejected the true Messiah. This Antichrist will be raised from the dead just as Jesus was. And when the unbelieving hoards witness this resurrection, they willingly give their worship and allegiance to this son of Satan.

> **The whole world was astonished and followed the Beast (Antichrist).**
> **Men worshipped the dragon (Satan) because he had given authority to the Beast, and they also worshipped the Beast.**
>
> *Revelation 13:3,4*

So this man will become the greatest dictator the world has ever seen. He will openly slander God and Jesus Christ and will hunt down those people who turn to God in these days and will kill many of them because of their faith. He will be assisted in this by a second beast who is the False Prophet. As the Antichrist is a political leader so the False Prophet will be a religious leader. He will be empowered by Satan to do many lying signs and wonders so that he might deceive the inhabitants of the earth. He will have such magic power that he will perform a miracle that will truly dazzle and amaze the populace.

> **He ordered them to set up an image to the Beast (Antichrist) who was wounded by the sword and yet lived.**
> **He was given power to give breath to the image of the first beast so that it could speak and cause all who refused to worship the image to be killed.** *Revelation 13:14,15*

Is it any wonder that the unbelieving people of the world will give their allegiance to this man? For this scripture tells us that the False Prophet will have the power to make images of the Antichrist come to life and speak. This image could be a statue or a picture of the Antichrist. Those believers who are not deceived but turn to God, they will be put to death for refusing to bow down to the image of the Beast. Furthermore, this False Prophet, who works in tandem with his boss, the Antichrist, puts into operation a system designed to ostracize all those who refuse to accept his sovereignty.

> **He also forced everyone, small and great, rich and poor, free and slave, to receive a mark on his right hand or on his forehead,**
> **so that no one could buy or sell unless he had the mark, which is the name of the beast or the number of his name.**
> **This calls for wisdom. If anyone has insight let him calculate the number of the Beast, for it is a man's number. His number is 666.**
> *Revelation 13:16-18*

In other words, the Antichrist and his government are going to form a club. If you are not in this club then you will be boycotted. You will not be able to buy or sell or do business unless you join this club. In order to get into the club you must take this brand either in your right hand or on your forehead.

The above verse states that this system of accounting employed by the Antichrist, will be able to keep track of the buying and selling of everyone in the whole world. Is it not amazing to you that this verse was written almost 2000 years ago, yet only in the last few recent years have we got the technology to put this into practical application? Surely this is a powerful sign that we are approaching the fulfilment of these very words when we see them become a reality before our eyes.

Many observers believe that this brand or mark will be a microchip inserted just under the skin.

As I write there are advertisements on TV encouraging people to use 'laser' cards instead of cash. More and more the use of cash is being replaced by plastic cards. Up until recent times the idea of putting a mark on people to keep track of their buying and selling would seem far fetched. But not now. You can do financial transactions in one country and they appear on a computer screen in another country fifteen seconds later. The use of plastic is a feature of our everyday life now and in every country plastic is being introduced and cash is being replaced.

Financial gurus know we are destined for a 'cashless society'. Plastic is so much more sensible and does away with many cash transactions. But plastic cards can be cumbersome too. You can lose them, you can break them or they can be stolen. But the thing that makes the card work is the tiny microchip in it. It holds all the information in that little chip. Your date of birth, your credit rating. So to save all the trouble associated with the plastic card, we simply take the chip and insert it just under the skin of the right hand. Bingo. Now you can't lose it! We cannot say for sure if this is the 'mark of the beast' that will apply during the seven years of Great Tribulation. We are merely observing the way society is going and postulating that this may be the case. The people who are to go through these times will know when it occurs. But anybody who does accept this mark is inviting eternal damnation. For we are warned in no uncertain terms of the consequences of this choice.

> **If anyone worships the Beast and his image and receives his mark on the forehead or on the hand, he too will drink of the wine of God's fury, which has been poured full strength into the cup of His wrath.**
> **He will be tormented with burning sulphur in the presence of the holy angels and of the lamb.**
> **And the smoke of their torment rises for ever and ever.**
> **There is no rest day or night for those who worship the Beast and his image, or for anyone who receives the mark of his name.**
> *Revelation 14:9-11*

It is going to be a hard choice, for if you do not accept this mark then you cannot buy anything. This means people who find themselves in this situation must forage for themselves. They must grow their own food and provide for their own well-being and that of their families. They will have to learn self sufficiency and survival very fast in order to have a chance of making it through the seven years. On top of having to survive without being able to buy or sell or do business, people will have to contend with the wrath of Satan, for it is prophesied that he will hunt down and kill many of these good people. But there is hope, for God promises to help those who endure to the end.

It is a stark choice. You can accept the mark and enjoy the benefits for a short season, or refuse the mark and risk losing your life. But you will ultimately reap the rewards of everlasting glory if you stick it out to the end. So there is really only one choice to make. Let that choice be life, for receiving this mark is not as innocuous as it may appear. Apparently, you are not just making a trivial business decision. Whoever accepts this mark is pledging allegiance to the Antichrist and to Satan who gives him his power. Once you make this decision, there will be no going back. The majority of the world will accept this mark wholeheartedly. Not only will they openly worship the Antichrist but they will give themselves totally to Satan and will openly worship him as well.

And even when the people of God are being murdered because they refuse to accept this mark, the rest of the world will endorse and support the killings. How great is the grace of God that you can have the opportunity to avoid these terrible times before they occur. All you have to do is believe in God and in His Son and you shall be saved from this terrible hell. Put your trust in Him and you will not be disappointed.

Final Countdown

IN THE MID 1930S, Hitler used his time to build up an arsenal bigger than any other ever seen. He built fighter planes and bombers. His panzer tanks were more powerful and faster than anything ever built. In a very short amount of time he had a military force capable of (almost) conquering most of the world. Many political activists, who watched as he built up his military machine, demanded action. They argued that if they did not arm themselves likewise, their security could be in danger. Of course the liberals in the governments warned against such a reaction. They said that if we begin to build up arms, it will only escalate the chances of war. So they took no action. As soon as he was ready, Hitler overran Poland without hardly having to fire a shot. He continued to invade and conquer with ease, breaking all his peace treaties in so doing. By the time all the rest of the world got involved and he was finally stopped, up to 70 million people were dead.

The last half of the seven years of the Great Tribulation, will make the first and second world wars look like a minor side show. All the major players are arming themselves to the teeth in preparation for this final conflict. The stage is set. The players are making final adjustments. It is only a matter of time.

We are told in *Ezekiel 38* and *39* that a '**great power from the**

North' will attack Jerusalem. If you examine a map you will see that the great power north of Palestine is Russia. Many scholars agree that it is Russia, together with an alliance of Moslem nations, which will combine to make this assault. This will happen sometime during the mid point of the Great Tribulation. It will come as a complete surprise to Israel who will be dwelling safely in peace at this point. For we are told that the Antichrist will broker a peace agreement between Israel and her Arab neighbours guaranteeing Israel protection (*Daniel 7:27*). This marks the beginning of the seven years of Tribulation.

Because Israel is not expecting an invasion, there will be a sort of pseudo peace during the initial stages of the seven years. But at some point the **'great power from the north'** together with the **'king of the south'** will decide to launch a surprise attack. In so doing, they catch everyone unawares and their incursion is successful. However, according to Ezekiel, God will destroy these armies in the hills north of Jerusalem. But not before they have plundered Jerusalem, slaughtering two-thirds of the inhabitants. The remaining one-third escape into the desert. When these armies retreat to the hills north of Jerusalem, they are then destroyed and utterly routed (probably by the Antichrist and his Western alliance). The peace treaty that was brokered by the Antichrist is now broken. At this stage this dictator has been raised from the dead and is totally empowered by Satan. The Russian and Moslem armies having been defeated, the Antichrist with the military might of the West behind him, moves into the power vacuum that now exists in the Middle East. He sets up camp in Jerusalem at this point in time and the Temple will have been rebuilt as was prophesied. The Antichrist will then fulfil another prophecy by entering into the Temple and setting himself up as the true Messiah, demanding worship for himself and speaking blasphemies against the God of heaven.

He shall speak great words against the most high, and shall wear

> **out the saints of the most high, and think to change times and laws.** *Daniel 7:25*

> **He shall do according to his will and shall exalt himself above every God, and shall speak marvellous things against the God of Gods.** *Daniel 11:36*

In the New Testament, we have Paul's corroboration of Daniel's words.

> **He will oppose and will exalt himself over everything that is called God or is worshipped, so that he sets himself up in God's temple, proclaiming himself to be God.**
> **The coming of the lawless one will be in accordance with the work of Satan, displayed in all kinds of counterfeit miracles, signs and wonders.** *II Thessalonians 2:4,9*

While this is going on, the 'Kings of the East' decide to make their move. This is the first time in the Bible that the people of Asia and the Far East are ever mentioned, yet we are told that an army numbering 200 million will massacre one third of the population of the world as they cut a swathe westward.

Never before has the Bible referred to any great powers either from the North or the Far East until these end-time scenarios. It is only in recent years that either China or Russia have become superpowers with nuclear weapons and arsenals capable of mass destruction. Again we marvel at the accuracy of prophecy as we see these players align themselves to fulfil their destiny.

The great River Euphrates has always been the dividing line between the Middle East and China and the Far East. We are told that this great river is dried up to make way for this 200-million-strong army. The Euphrates is 1,700 miles long. This huge army continues southwest with Palestine as its destination. Conflict with the Antichrist and his Western powers seems inevitable.

The Antichrist is to receive his authority from a confederation of ten nations. Most scholars of end-time prophecy believe this confederacy will be made up of the remnants of the revived Roman Empire. Seeing as the United States is largely made up of European people who are descended from the old Roman Empire, it is feasible and probable that they would be part of a military alliance with Europe and other Western nations.

The EU is fast becoming the strongest financial and military block in the world. Along with the United States and every other world power, oil is essential to keep the wheels of industry turning. Anything that may interfere with or threaten their oil supply would have to be dealt with.

It is for this reason that the Americans, along with all the other allied nations, moved so quickly into the Gulf War. As one pundit put it, 'if they were growing carrots in Kuwait, the Iraqis would still be there'.

The world is aligning itself into four main power blocks. On one side you have the Russian people who are ideologically and religiously close to another main power, the Moslems. Both dislike and distrust the West, particularly America. Whenever an international incident occurs the Russians always side with the Arab nations and vice versa.

It is also economically and politically expedient for Russia to ally themselves to their Moslem neighbours who are rich in oil dollars, as their own economy is not healthy. In exchange for cash and oil, the Russians exchange military hardware and know how.

Russia still maintains a vast nuclear arsenal. A US air force pilot who was detailed to do reconnaissance over the North Pole thought that he would have an easy term of duty, due to the condition of the Soviet economy, but he and his team were on their toes 24 hours a day, trying to keep track of Russian nuclear submarines doing manoeuvres under the ice of the polar cap.

The Russians have a large fleet of nuclear submarines, each with 200 nuclear warheads, capable of destroying thousands of cities and millions of lives. And these missiles can reach their targets in a matter of minutes.

China has the capability now of hitting targets in the West. India and Pakistan have recently become nuclear powers and have been rattling their sabres at one another. India has a population of 800 million. China with 1200 million, have been cultivating closer links with Japan and other Asian neighbours. The threat from the 'Kings of the East' may be a confederacy of these nations as they eye the oil of the Middle East. This is the third major power block, Russia and the Arab nations being the other two.

Then there is the West. Together with the United States, Europe is possibly the most formidable of the super powers as she continues to expand, taking in Eastern European countries. The EU is becoming the richest economic trading force in the world and is consolidating its military strategy.

So there are four main power blocks. We are told that God will gather all the armies of the world to battle in this area of the Middle East. The Valley of Megiddo forms a land bridge between three continents. During the final three and a half years of this time of trouble, many will die from all the other minor wars, famines, diseases and general breakdown in society that will occur. But it is in Armageddon that the final button will be pushed to plunge the world into the eve of destruction.

There is no way these countries will stand by and allow anything to threaten their oil flow. This is why I believe it is reasonable to assume that a huge military force will gather in the Middle East to be confronted with the threat posed by the 200 million strong army arriving from the East. There can be only one outcome to this stand off. All out war.

The prophet Zechariah, writing in 410 BC, wrote of this day:

> **Behold the day of the Lord comes when I will gather all nations against Jerusalem to battle ... then shall the Lord go forth and fight against those nations.** *Zechariah 14:1-3*

Earlier I wrote of some of the descriptions of John as he tried to portray a picture of the visions that he both saw and heard. He spoke of a vision that sounds like it might be military aircraft with *'breastplates of iron and the sound of their wings was like the sound of many horses and chariots rushing into battle'*. And *'out of their mouths came fire, smoke and sulphur and a third of mankind was killed by the three plagues of fire, smoke and sulphur ...'* We also spoke of the 'Wormwood' which will fall into one third of all drinking water, polluting it and causing death to all who drink it. Could this be biological warfare? Or could it be as a result of nuclear fallout?

In the above quotation we are told that one-third of the population of the world will be killed by what John calls three plagues of fire, brimstone and sulphur. I am convinced that he is describing three nuclear strikes. The first strike will be when the Russians, along with their Moslem comrades, are destroyed in the mountains north of Israel by the Antichrist and his powerful western alliance.

The second will be the nuclear power that the 200-million-strong armies of the East use as they slaughter all before them in their drive towards the Middle East. The third and final nuclear strike will also be the seventh and last of the Seals, Trumpets and Vial judgements.

At the end of the seven years of Great Tribulation, the vast army from the East will have arrived at the Valley of Megiddo. Here they will be confronted by the rich and powerful military alliance from the West led by the Antichrist. There is a stand-off. John describes what will happen.

> **Then they gathered the kings together in the place that in Hebrew is called Armageddon.**
> **Then there came flashes of lightning, rumblings, peals of thunder and a severe earthquake. No earthquake has ever occurred since man has been on earth, so tremendous was the quake.**
> **The great city split into three parts, and the cities of the nations collapsed.** *Revelation 16:16,18,19*

After all these vast armies are gathered, there is a moment's hesitation, then someone pushes the button to release the first nuclear missile. With that a chain reaction starts which cannot be stopped. All the submarines on both sides launch their deadly cargo. Land-based missiles from all sectors of the world are automatically fired. Hundreds and thousands of missiles are fired simultaneously and pass each other in the air. This is why John describes it as:

Flashes of lightning ... just like the images we see on television as we witness missiles and huge cannons firing into the blackness of night;

Rumblings ... the sound of distant explosions as the bombs hit their targets;

Peals of thunder ... caused by the initial firing of the weapons and their impact when they hit;

And a severe earthquake like no other ... The words 'nuclear strike' or 'explosions' were not in John's vocabulary. So when he saw all the missilies hit their targets, he could only describe it as a 'tremendous earthquake'.

And the cities of the nations collapsed ... just as Hiroshima and Nagasaki collapsed 50 years ago. There is only one thing that can cause all the cities of the nations to collapse at the same time. John is describing a nuclear strike. This is Armageddon. The history of the world is the history of war.

I can say for sure that this is exactly what is going to happen. It is said in the Bible that all wars and famine and death and sickness are caused by the devil and Satan (*Hebrews 2:14*). It is the agency of an evil spirit working through people and through physical catastrophes that result in death and destruction. Even though it appears that man is the cause and maker of war, the real power lies with the invisible spiritual influences that are manipulating situations and pulling the strings in the background.

Jesus Christ is coming back to finish the battle and establish His reign on this earth for 1,000 years.

He is returning not on an ass as He did before, but on a

white horse as a military leader and He is going to exact revenge on His enemies and the enemies of God.

> **I saw heaven standing open, and there before me was a white horse, whose rider is called faithful and true. With justice he judges and makes war.**
> **The armies of heaven were following him, riding on white horses and dressed in fine linen, white and clean.**
> **On his robe and on his thigh he has this name written: King of Kings and Lord of Lords.** *Revelation 19:11-16*

Then Jesus goes forth to do battle against the Beast and the False Prophet. These two are captured and are thrown alive into the lake of burning sulphur. All the flesh eating birds are then invited to come and eat the flesh of all those that are killed, and the birds gorge themselves on their flesh. Then the dragon, the ancient serpent, who is the devil, or Satan, is bound and cast into the abyss for 1,000 years. At the end of the 1,000 years he must be set free for a short time.

When the Lord Jesus lands on the Mount of Olives, the mountain will split in two. Half will move towards the north and half towards the south. Then fresh water will gush forth from under the Mount and will flow half to the eastern sea and half to the western (*Zechariah 14:4,8*). Then Jesus will begin to establish His kingdom. Only then will we see the fulfilment of the prophetic prayer called the Lord's prayer.

> **Thy kingdom come, thy will be done on earth, as it is in heaven.**

Those that were martyred because of their faith during the Great Tribulation will be resurrected to reign with Christ for 1,000 years. It will take seven months to burn the weapons that are left over after the final holocaust. But then we begin a reign of peace. Then, all will be worthwhile as we enter Paradise regained.

Garden of Delights

EVER WONDER WHAT IT might be like to live in a hassle-free world? No more having to compete in the workplace, no more worry about bills, violence, murder, rape. Not having to put up with bad weather and bad news. A world where you don't have to worry about your kids' safety or their future. A place where everyone loves everyone else and there is abundance of food and long life. No more wars, no more starvation or famine, no more inequality and injustice. Well, you've come to the right place.

When Jesus Christ comes back to establish His kingdom, the world will enter a blessed period for 1,000 years. It will be Paradise regained. The Hebrew word for *'Eden'* in *The Book of Genesis* means *'garden of delights'*. Paradise is only mentioned three times in the Bible and it is always a place on the earth. It has nothing to do with heaven. When Jesus comes back to reign we will be entering Paradise. This future kingdom will be ruled by Jesus Christ and He will rule it with a rod of iron, which means He will rule with real justice.

When Jesus was dying on the cross, we are told that three out of the four who were crucified with him railed against Him and said *'if you are the Son of God, then why don't you get yourself out of this situation?'* and they cursed Him. But the fourth man told them to shut up, and said to Jesus **'remember me when you**

come into your kingdom' (*Mark 23:40-42*). Then Jesus told him that he would be with Him in Paradise. (Please note there were four men crucified with Jesus not two, but that's another story).

Those of us who are saved will be with Jesus in this Paradise kingdom along with believers (saints) who do not succumb to the mark of the Beast and survive the Great Tribulation. The believers who are killed by the Antichrist during the seven years will be resurrected and will reign with Christ for 1,000 years. Also, those Jewish saints from the Old Testament will be resurrected and will also be present in this millennial kingdom. It will be our job to put the earth back in order after the devastation caused by the holocaust of the seven years of Tribulation. We are given lots of details about this period in the Old Testament. For instance, there will be no more war in this glorious time, for men will '**beat their swords into ploughshares and their spears into pruning hooks. Nation will not take up sword against nation, nor will they train for war anymore**' (*Isaiah 2:4*).

Look at all the billions that are currently spent on arms and maintaining defence forces. This will be no more for we will now use our energies to cultivate food for everyone. And boy, will there be an abundance of food.

> **'The days are coming', declares the Lord,**
> **'When the reaper will be overtaken by the ploughman and the planter by the one treading grapes. New wine will drip from the mountains and flow from all the hills.'**
>
> *Amos 9:13*

In other words, there will be so much food, year in year out, that when one man is still gathering the crops, the next guy is coming to start ploughing again. So we will have no need to worry about where the next meal is coming from. Famine and starvation will be no more. There will be a change in the atmosphere and in the soil and the animal and plant kingdom. Isaiah tells us of this future 'Garden of Delights'.

The wolf will live with the lamb, the leopard will lie down with the goat.
The calf and the lion and the yearling together: and a little child will lead them.
The cow will feed with the bear, their young will lie down together, and the lion will eat straw like the ox.
The infant will play near the hole of the cobra, and the young child put his hand into the viper's nest.
They will neither harm nor destroy on all my holy mountain, for the earth will be full of the knowledge of the Lord as the waters cover the sea. *Isaiah 11:6-9*

Sounds like a nice place to be! We are told that life will be a lot longer than at present. For if one dies at the age of 100, it will be regarded as dying young. It is not going to be totally perfect there as we are informed that Jesus will rule with a *'rod of iron'*. This would imply that some people will step out of line on occasion. However, the overall picture is one of a blessed existence of peace and prosperity with Jesus Christ ruling from His headquarters in Jerusalem. When He returns to this earth to live and reign for 1,000 years, then those promises He made during His first coming will be realised.

Blessed are the pure in spirit, for theirs is the kingdom of heaven.
Blessed are those who mourn, for they will be comforted.
Blessed are the meek, for they will inherit the earth.
Blessed are those who hunger and thirst for righteousness, for they will be filled.
Blessed are the merciful, for they will be shown mercy.
Blessed are the pure in heart, for they will see God.
Blessed are the peacemakers, for they will be called the sons of God.
Blessed are those who are persecuted because of righteousness, for theirs is the kingdom of heaven. *Matthew 5:3-10*

Interestingly, further on in this same chapter Jesus makes an informative statement.

For I tell you that unless your righteousness surpasses that of

> **the Pharisees and the Teachers of the law, you will certainly not enter the kingdom of heaven.** *Matthew 5:20*

We were always taught that when you die you go to heaven or hell. But this is not true. When the Lord comes back to take away the believers at the Rapture, then we who are alive will go to this place called heaven for a seven-year hiatus while the Great Tribulation takes place. All those Christians who have been dead since Pentecost will be raised and will be there too. But the future for us and for the rest of mankind is here on earth, first in the 1,000 year kingdom of Christ, and later in a New Heaven and New Earth. So He is coming back here to reign. Our future is on planet earth, but in an infinitely improved state.

> **Eye has not seen nor ear heard, neither has it entered into the heart of man, the things that God has prepared for those that love him.** *I Corinthians 2:9*

During this 1,000 year period, Satan is bound and no longer free to deceive the nations. Over time the population grows exceedingly. And at the end of the 1,000 years, Satan is released for a short time. Now an amazing thing happens, for he manages to corrupt a huge number of the people who live during this time, and deceive them into attacking the camp of God's people. We are given very little information about this period so we cannot comment much upon it. However, is it not amazing that after living in a veritable Paradise for 1,000 years of bliss under the rule of the Son of God, that man could once again rebel and choose to reject God and His Messiah? This illustrates the utter depravity and evil of the human heart. But we should not be surprised at this situation, for Adam and Eve lived in a perfect world but they made a free will decision to disobey God. Also, before Lucifer fell he was the 'anointed cherub' *(Ezekiel 28:14*) and he 'walked in the Garden of God and was perfect' (*Ezekiel 28:13*), yet by his free will he chose to rebel against the most high God. So people during this 1,000 years will live in a near-perfect Paradise, but they will still have free will and therefore will be responsible for their actions and decisions. When this multitude attack they are consumed by fire from heaven which devours them. Then the devil, who deceived them, is thrown into the lake of burning sulphur where the Beast and the False Prophet had been thrown 1,000 years earlier (*Revelation 20:7-10)*.

After this there are what is called the 'Great White Throne' judgements. All the dead are judged here. Whoever's name is not found written in the Book of Life, is thrown into the lake of fire. The last two chapters of *Revelation* describe a New Heaven and a New Earth. God himself, our Father, is coming to live with Jesus His Son and with us in this New Eternal Kingdom. All of history which has gone before, from the time before Adam to the days of Jesus until now, are a mere preface to that day in the future when God will be joined with His family. Then He will be with His sons and daughters who chose to love Him by their own free will. He will have then what every father wants, children to share His love with.

> **Then I saw a new heaven and a new earth, for the first heaven and the first earth had passed away, and there was no longer any sea.**
> **I saw the Holy City, the new Jerusalem, coming down out of heaven from God, prepared as a bride beautifully dressed for her husband.**
> **And I heard a loud voice from the throne saying, 'Now the dwelling of God is with men, and he will live with them. They will be his people, and God himself will be with them and be their God.**
> **He will wipe every tear from their eyes. There will be no more death or mourning or crying or pain, for the old order of things has passed away.'** *Revelation 21:1-4*

Oh, what a glorious day that will be. Do you want to be there? All the pain and all the tears and heartache and suffering of this life will be forgotten when we reach this future day.

> **For I reckon that the sufferings of this present time are not worthy to be compared with the glory which shall be revealed to us.**
> *Romans 8:18*

This is the good news. This is what we have to look forward to. This is why Jesus suffered and died and rose again. So that you and I might live. What fun and joy lies ahead for those of us who believe and await His return with patience. Only those whose names are written in the Book of Life will enjoy this future Paradise. Very few are chosen by the grace of God. Make sure your name is included so that you too can enjoy life eternal with God and His Son.

> **The desert and the parched land will be glad; the wilderness will rejoice and blossom. Like the crocus, it will burst into bloom; it will rejoice greatly and shout for joy. The glory of Lebanon will be given to it, the splendour of Carmel and Sharon; they will see the glory of the Lord, the splendour of our God. Strengthen the feeble hands, steady the knees that give way; say to those with fearful hearts, 'Be strong, do not fear; your God will come, he will come with vengeance; with divine retribution he will come to save you'. Then will the eyes of the blind be opened and the ears of the deaf unstopped. Then will the lame leap like a deer, and the mute tongue shout for joy. Water will gush forth in the wilderness and streams in the desert. The burning sand will become a pool, the thirsty ground bubbling springs. In the haunts where jackals once lay, grass and reeds and papyrus will grow. And a highway will be there; it will be called the Way of Holiness. The unclean will not journey on it; it will be for those who walk in that Way; wicked fools will not go about on it. No lion will be there, nor will any ferocious beast get up on it; they will not be found there. But only the redeemed will walk there, and the ransomed of the Lord will return. They will enter Zion with singing, everlasting joy will overtake them, and sorrow and sighing will flee away.**
>
> *Isaiah 35:1-10*

Did Time Make the Clock?

SCIENTISTS ARE THE HIGH priests of solemn truth in our day. If a scientist said it, then it must be true. There is one subject that probably did more to convince people that the Bible is a fable more than any other – the Theory of Evolution.

This theory is almost universally accepted as being the truth regarding where we came from. Even though thousands of secular scientists will admit that there is little or no proof of authenticity in the theory, yet the ordinary layman still remains convinced. Why? Because this is all he has been taught.

Briefly speaking, the theory of evolution says that there was a mixture of methane, water vapour and ammonia. There was an explosion or 'Big Bang' out of which all life as we know it today emerged or evolved. They call this 'spontaneous generation'. In other words, we basically evolved from nothing. Some scientists say this explosion occurred 30 or 40 million years ago. Others say it occurred four and a half billion years ago.

By definition, science is the study of facts under controlled circumstances. Another way of saying it is that science is observable evidence. But the theory of evolution is not based on observable evidence, for no scientist was around to observe exactly what happened. This means that evolution is an assumption and is in no way scientific. So if it is an assumption, then it requires a leap of faith to believe in it. Therefore the theory of evolution is a belief system based on faith and is thus a religious belief.

Spontaneous generation would have us believe that life came from non-life. From nothing came everything. Yet we have never seen, for instance, a machine originate from nothing or by chance. Look around you at the things that have been made by man. We may not understand how they work, but we know that there is an intelligence behind them. The same goes for much of the technology around us today, from cyber space to fibre optics. We do not know how they work, but we know it was not by chance.

A scientist in the seventeenth century said he could create mice by spontaneous generation. This was his proof: take one old, sweaty shirt. Shake a handful of wheat all over the shirt then leave it in a shed for 21 days. When you come back, there are mice all over the shirt. This proves that mice evolve by spontaneous generation!

We laugh at the stupidity of such findings today yet many people believe that this is exactly how man and everything around us today came into being. Take some gases and liquids: leave them alone for between 30 million years to four-and-a-half billion years; then when you come back, bingo, you have life in all its wonderful diversification from humans to plants to animals to fish to birds, etc. And how did all these billions and trillions of life forms come into being? Evolution via spontaneous generation.

Is there any scientific facts to verify this? No, not one, but we don't believe in God so there must be some other explanation!

In *Genesis* we are told that God created the heavens and the earth and all that is in them. How did He do it? I don't know. In order to explain that, I would have to be bigger than God, and that I am not. Henry understood the Ford but the Ford did not understand Henry.

Charles Darwin is credited with the origin of the theory of evolution but there is some proof that he stole the idea from a man who was on his death bed as he travelled in the Far East. He returned to England, expanded the theory and claimed it for his own. If this is true then this makes Darwin a thief and a liar, but irrespective of this, his theory just does not hold water.

Ever notice in books on evolution that they have sketches of monkeys on all fours, then progressing onto their hind feet, and as they walk they metamorphose into a fully-fledged man? You will see these sketches in museums all over the world beside the cases that hold examples of fossils of every kind. There are billions of fossils all over the world today. Everything from man to animal to fish to plants, even dinosaurs.

But there is something peculiar about all these fossils. Every one of them is perfectly formed, and complete. Not one fossil is 'evolving' from one state to another i.e., there is no fish with little feet on it. No bird with stumpy evolving wings. They are all perfectly formed fish and already fully-formed birds. This goes for every fossil in the world.

This fossil evidence is a great embarrassment to evolutionists. Even Darwin himself said that without one piece of fossil evidence as proof, his theory was no more than worthless speculation. So, if evolution is true, we should find millions of fossils showing the slow evolution from one stage to another. But the evidence is we have no intermediate types, either fossilised or living thus proving that the theory is no more than speculation.

So what does the evidence that we do have, point to? What do these millions of fossils prove? These would seem to suggest that there was some huge cataclysmic event which suddenly befell the earth. This holocaust was so sudden and so severe that it buried millions of animals, plants, humans, etc., and froze them in rocks in a moment of time, capturing a snapshot of history.

Is there such an event recorded that would fit with this evidence/description? There certainly is. It was the flood of Noah.

This deluge was so cataclysmic that it wiped every living thing off the face of the earth, except for what was in the boat.

But why don't scientists acknowledge this possibility as an obvious explanation of fossils? Because they don't want to acknowledge that the Bible might be right. Otherwise creation must be right and all the other miracles must be right and the resurrection must be right and so on.

There is mounting evidence that the ark did indeed exist. According to the record in *Genesis 8* the boat landed on Mount Ararat which today is in eastern Turkey. Huge anchor stones have been found in this area, eleven in all, which were used as ballast to keep the Ark steady as it floated. The Turkish government have stopped excavation on a site which many believe contain the buried hull of the ark. But science will not concur with these findings because then they will have to agree that the flood was a judgement against the world at the time of Noah as was the destruction of Sodom and Gomorrah. Also the events prophesied in *The Book of Revelations* is a judgement against mankind because of their rejection of the Messiah and their embracing and worship of Satan. And this earth is fast ripening for judgement.

According to *Genesis* chapter seven, verse eleven:

> **In the six hundredth year of Noah's life, on the seventeenth day of the second month – on that day all the springs of the great deep burst forth, and the flood gates of the heavens were opened.**
> **And rain fell on the earth for forty days and forty nights.**

We are told that the earth was flooded, to a depth of twenty feet above the highest mountain, for one hundred and fifty days.

Noah was over one whole year on the ark with his family before the waters dried up. Every single living breathing thing was wiped out and buried in the deluge. And thus we have fossils today.

We saw television pictures of the devastation caused by a

few days of rain in Honduras and Nicaragua. Thousands of people were buried in mudslides and floods. Crops were washed away. 400,000 were made homeless. Two million people were affected. The country is in ruin.

If this can be caused by just a few days of rain, imagine the effects of 40 days and 40 nights of heavy downpour coupled with the springs of the great deep bursting forth.

The good news is that God promised that He would never allow the world to be flooded again.

So why is the theory of evolution so readily embraced? Because the god of this world wants to keep you in ignorance and away from the truths revealed in the Bible. Evolution provides a somewhat plausible explanation and because it's backed up by science, it makes the creation story seem invalid. If you believe in evolution, then you can use this to justify your actions. Both Hitler and Stalin believed in and were exponents of evolution. Because they believed in survival of the fittest, and that some humans are more highly evolved than others, they could justify the extermination of the weak and undesirable. They clinically exterminated millions in the name of evolution, so that the superior races could advance and they could dispose of the dross and the weak of the human race.

The truth is that the theory of evolution is not based on scientific evidence (observable facts) but is a religious belief system that has its basis in metaphysics, humanism and atheism: for it explains God away. The reason they have not found the missing link is because there is none. There never was one and they will never find one. It's all a hoax.

Look around you. Consider all the millions of life forms in all their beauty and glory – all fully formed and beautifully and wonderfully made. From the perfect markings of a trout to the splendour and majesty of the peacock. From the industry of the ant to the colossus that is the elephant. And you really believe that all this came from a supposed explosion that nobody saw? Where did the rocks evolve from? And the stars and the sun?

We may as well believe that mice evolve from a sweaty shirt sprinkled with oats as to believe in this unsubstantiated theory.

Postscript

1. Evolution is so unlikely that it is tantamount to a whirlwind blowing through a scrap yard and coming out as a Boeing 747 at the other end.
2. You have a frog in your hand. What is it? It is a frog. What will it be this time next year? A frog. What will it be in ten years? (By the natural process of procreation?) A frog. What will it be in 100 years? A frog. What will it be in 30 million years? Eh ... Marilyn Monroe!!?!

Addendum

But what about dinosaurs and prehistoric man, I hear you ask. These fit into the gap between *Genesis 1:1* and *1: 2*. In the first verse of *Genesis* we are told:

> God in the beginning created the heavens and the earth.

Since God **is** perfect, therefore His creation must of necessity also be perfect. But in verse two, something has happened:

> **And the Earth became without form and void and darkness was upon the face of the deep.**

The Hebrew word for 'without form' is *tohú* which means 'waste'. The earth became 'waste and void'. It was not created that way for we are told in *Isaiah 45:18* that God did not create the earth *tohú* (waste). So something happened between verse one and verse two which rendered the earth 'waste and void'. We are not told what happened, how it happened or how many years elapsed. Perhaps it was millions. So you can have all the cavemen and dinosaurs you want on the earth in *Genesis 1:1*. Then something cataclysmic happened which obliterated the earth, killing everything and rendering it totally 'waste and void'.

It was later on that God went to work and put the world, as we know it, back in order in six days. This creation is recorded in the first few chapters of *Genesis*.

Written in the Stars

THERE IS A SMALL TOWN in the state of Colorado in the United States of America called Irwin. When it was a mining town in the 1800s it was called Ruby Camp. The silver mined there was a sulfide of silver in crystal form. When this was crushed it became a blood red colour; thus the name 'Ruby Camp'. In the spring of 1879, a wagon driver brought in supplies from the railroad. It was early when he finished his work. He did not have to leave until the following morning so he told some of the miners that he would like to do a little prospecting for himself. They decided to pull his leg and told him to go down the little gully nearby and start digging.

He went down and began digging. The miners who played the joke on him began laughing at his naivety. After digging a while the wagon driver noticed a vein of silver. After some more work he discovered that this silver vein was quite substantial. Soon afterwards he sold the vein, which he named 'Forrest Queen Mine' for $50,000 which was a fortune back then. Within two years the new owners had taken out silver ore worth one million dollars.

Hundreds of miners had walked over this mine. Not one of them realised the great wealth and potential riches that was right under their noses – not until the wagon driver had begun digging a few hundred yards from the place where he sought advice. The Word of God is like this mine. It is full of the riches and treasures of God. But it has rarely been mined. So very few discover its wealth. In order to understand the Word of God you must have the Spirit of God. Otherwise it is just words to the natural man.

> **But the natural man receives not the things of the Spirit of God, for they are foolishness unto him: neither can he know them because they are spiritually discerned.** *1 Corinthians 2:14*

The 'natural man' is without the Spirit of God and therefore goes by his five senses. He will never understand and cannot receive the things of the Spirit. I would not criticise a blind man for not being able to appreciate a work of art. So why criticise the natural man for not appreciating the Word of God? Remember what Christ said as he hung on the cross, *'Forgive them Father; for they know not what they do'*.

The writer, W.W. Kinsley, in describing the masterpiece of God's Word, wrote:

> *The more profoundly phenomena have been studied by scientist and scientific philosophers the more gloriously have shown out the truths ... that God has busied himself through untold ages in preparing for man's advent, that man has been the great goal of his endeavour, the ultimate Thule of his creative thought on this planet; that all this prolonged preparation could not have been merely to render comfortable a short-lived and low planned animal existence; that this patient approach could not have been to a consummation so inconsequential and unworthy ...*

Man was not born to just die. Everything that we are and have around us is for a purpose. We are not here because of blind chance. Only when you begin to mine the great treasures of God's Word will you discover the reason for life, and the meaning of life. Everything else is vanity and will soon be forgotten.

For 2,500 years, the Word of God was not written down. Only until Moses, *circa* 1490 BC, was the written Word begun. So how did God preserve his truth until that time and communicate it to his people? The answer: it was written in the stars. There is a divinely designed system and order to God's creation. He numbered and named the stars.

> **He determines the number of the stars and calls them each by name.** *Psalm 147:4*

In the beginning, when God created the heavens and the earth and set the stars in their courses, he gave specific names to the stars. These names and their groupings reveal the whole story of God's plan of redemption. This information and knowledge was given to Adam who in turn taught it to the Patriarchs and in this manner it was passed on from generation to generation throughout the centuries.

> **And God said, 'Let there be lights in the expanse of the sky to separate the day from the night, and let them serve as signs to mark seasons and days and years.**
> **And let them be lights in the expanse of the sky to give light on the earth.'** *Genesis 1:14,15*

In this first mention of the stars in the sky, God made it clear that as well as giving light upon the earth, that the stars were for '*signs*' and for 'seasons' and for days and years. The Magi that followed the star of Bethlehem were astronomers. They understood the ancient meanings of the stars and thus knew that the Messiah was born by what happened in the stars at that time. It is not said that there were three wise men from the East. There may have been six or ten. These were probably from the area of Persia where the knowledge of astronomy was passed down from the days of Daniel's captivity in Babylon. The stars had signalled the birth of the Messiah for it was written in the stars.

I recently heard one of the astronauts who first walked on the moon speak of his awe at seeing the world from space for the first time. He described the beautiful hue and colours that reflected in the light and told of how the earth just hung there in space as if by some invisible chord. He said its majesty resembled a precious jewel.

A well-known astronomer was discussing with his son the influence of the heavenly bodies on the earth. This is what the astronomer said to his son:

> *I have noticed that at certain times the Earth is lifted out of her orbit or path by an unseen body lying beyond the reach of our most powerful telescope. If ever they build a larger telescope, I wish you would go and search the heavens to find out what it is that so affects this planet of ours.*
>
> He then goes on to say,
>
> *'When the great Lick Observatory was reared with its powerful telescope this son travelled across sea and continent, and one clear night turned the great telescope against the dark space in the heavens where this unseen, uncharted planet reached down its mighty hand and gripped the Earth. After gazing a while, suddenly there appeared a tiny speck of light. It was a star swinging in its giant orbit away out on the frontier of the Universe. He saw the planet that had so strangely affected the earth. It was millions of miles beyond the farthest star that the human eye had ever seen. Yet this giant star sweeping on its great orbit came regularly every few years close enough to our planet, so that it could reach its mighty hand of gravitation down through the unmeasured space and grip our little earth and lift it out of its orbit. As a ship on the ocean responds to the slightest touch of the helm, our Earth responds to the touch of that distant sentinel and veers swiftly out of its course; then when the planet's grip is loosed, back into its path it comes and goes rhythmically on its way. This established one fact: that there is neither planet, nor sun, nor moon, nor star in all the vast universe but has its influence upon this little planet of ours.*
>
> *How it thrills the heart to realise that this Earth of ours, so small*

that 1,000 of them can be lost in the sun, is the centre and reason for the Universe. Tonight this old Earth of ours is being held as safely in the embrace of those uncounted and uncharted planets as a child in its mother's arms. The heavens are tonight Earth's only perfect timepiece, no watch or clock ever built by man can give us perfect time; but he who knows the path of the stars knows that every star, or sun, or planet will pass a certain given point in the great unpathed space on schedule time. The star may not have been seen for thousands of years, but she will appear at the cross-roads of the heavens not one second ahead nor one second behind her schedule.

Oh! The wonder of the Architect, the marvel of the Creator, the might of the Sustainer of this great universe of ours! If the Earth is the reason for the stellar heavens, what is the reason for the Earth? Before the Morning Stars sang their first anthem to the heart of the lonely Father God, before the foundations of the Earth were laid, before the first rays of light ever passed through the dark expanse, the heart of the great Creator God had a yearning, deep, mighty, eternal. It was the primordial passion for children. The Father heart of the Creator God longed for sons and daughters. This yearning passion took form, and God planned a universe for His Man, and in the heart of that universe He purposed a Home. There is no time with God. Time belongs to day and night, to sun and moon. The Omnipotent God was not hampered by days, nor nights, nor years. When Love laid the foundations of this mighty universe, He planned, He purposed it all to be the Home of His Man. It was to be Man's birthplace, Man's Garden of Delight, Man's University where he would learn to know his Father God.

All the stars were numbered and named by God (*Psalm 147:4*). There are twelve signs of the Zodiac. The word Zodiac originally means 'degrees' or 'steps' which mark the stages of the sun's path through the heavens, corresponding with the twelve months of the year. These names and twelve signs go back to the foundation of the world. The original and first prophecy concerning the promised Messiah was in *Genesis 3:15* but for 2,500 years was not written down. So for all this time the whole story of man's redemption from *Genesis* to *Revelation* was preserved in the naming of the stars and their groupings in signs and constellations. Thus the truth was enshrined and written in the stars where no human could interfere with it. In later years when the Word was written down and the scriptures were recorded, the old truths were no longer needed, and the ancient astronomy began fading away.

The astrology we have today is a bastardisation of the original truths of astronomy which the Greeks and others took from tradition and turned them into their own mythologies. So what is the one great theme of the signs of the Zodiac and where do we begin in the circle of the twelve signs? The answer is in *Genesis 3:15* after the fall of Adam and Eve when God said to the serpent:

> **'And I will put enmity between you and the woman, and between your seed and hers.**
> **He will crush your head and you will bruise his heel.'**

This is the first great promise and prophecy. God said that the seed of the woman (Christ) would crush the head of the serpent (Satan) but Satan would first bruise his heel (which was the crucifixion). This is the main theme of the whole written Word and of the signs of the Zodiac. But where do we begin to read this heavenly book? How are we to know the start of the story and its finish? The answer lies in the '*Sphinx*', for it bears the head of the woman '*Virgo*' and the body of the lion, 'Leo'. Thus the story begins with the Virgin and ends with the king 'Leo'. Of course the virgin is the sign for Mary and the king is the Messiah, Jesus Christ, who would ultimately crush the head of the serpent, '*Scorpio*'.

The word sphinx is from the Greek *sphingo* which means 'to join' because it ties together the two ends of the circle of the signs of the Zodiac.

There are twelve signs. In Bible numerology, twelve means 'governmental perfection' as in twelve apostles, twelve months of the year, twelve tribes of Israel, etc. So the twelve signs of the Zodiac are divided into three books of four chapters or signs each. Here is a brief summary of the twelve signs and their meanings, together with the names of the stars in their constellations*:

I VIRGO
The Prophecy of the Promised Seed
1. Coma: Woman and Child
2. Centaurus: The Despised Sin Offering
3. Bootes: The Coming One with Branch

II LIBRA
The Redeemed Atoning Work
1. Crux: The Cross Endured
2. Lupus: The Victim Slain
3. Corona: The Crown Bestowed

III SCORPIO
The Redeemer's Conflict
1. Serpens: Assaulting the Man's Heel
2. Ophiuchus: The Man Grasping the Serpent
3. Hercules: The Mighty Man Victorious

IV SAGITTARIUS
The Redeemed Triumph
1. Lura: Praise Prepared for the Conqueror
2. Ara: Fire Prepared for His Enemies
3. Draco: The Dragon Cast Down

V CAPRICORIUS
The Result of the Redeemer's Suffering
1. Sagitta: The Arrow of God Sent Forth
2. Aquila: The Smitten One Falling
3. Delphinus: The Dead One Rising Again

VI Aquarius

The Blessings Assured

1. Picis Australis: The Blessings Bestowed
2. Pegasus: The Blessings Quickly Coming
3. Cygnus: The Blesser Surely Returning

VII Pisces

The Blessings in Abeyance

1. The Band: The Great Enemy
2. Andromeda: The Redeemed in Bondage
3. Cepheus: The Deliverer Coming to Loosen

VII Aries

The Blessings Consummated

1. Cassiopeia: The Captive Delivered
2. Cetus: The Great Enemy Bound
3. Perseus The Breaker Delivering

IX Taurus

Messiah Coming to Rule

1. Orion: The Redeemer Breaking Forth As Light
2. Eridanus: Wrath Breaking Forth As A Flood
3. Auriga: Safety for His Redeemed in the Day of Wrath

X Gemini

Messiah As Prince of Princes

1. Lepus: The Enemy Trodden Underfoot
2. Canis Major: The Coming Glorious Prince
3. Canis Minor: The Exalted Redeemer

XI Cancer

Messiah's Redeemed Possessions

1. Ursa Minor: The Lesser Sheepfold
2. Ursa Major: The Fold and the Flock
3. Argo: The Pilgrims Arrival At Home

XII Leo
The Prophecy of Triumph Fulfilled
1. Hydra: The Old Serpent Destroyed
2. Crater: The Cup of Wrath Poured Out
3. Corvus: The Birds of Prey Devouring

* This is but a small summary of the greater truth which can be found in the work of E.W. Bullingers' *Witness of the Stars*.

As the star of Bethlehem, so called, proclaimed the arrival of the first coming of the Messiah, so too I believe the stars will announce his second advent. Oh, that we had an understanding of the ancient knowledge that we could read the signs.

> **The heavens declare the glory of God, the skies proclaim the work of His hands.**
> **Day after day they pour forth speech,**
> **Night after night they display knowledge.**
> **There is no speech of language**
> **Where their voice is not heard.**
> **Their voice goes out into all the earth,**
> **Their words to the ends of the world.**
> **In the heavens he has pitched a tent for the sun,**
> **Which is like a bridegroom coming forth from his pavilion,**
> **Like a champion rejoicing to run his course.**
> **It rises at one end of the heavens and makes its circuit to the other.**
> **Nothing is hidden from its heat.** *Psalm 19: 1-6*

Who is the Devil?

WHEN JESUS CHRIST CAME he exposed the devil. He turned over the rock, so to speak, and showed people the snake that was hiding underneath. He taught that there are two Gods: one is the true God and Father of all; the other is the god of this world, otherwise known as Satan, Lucifer, Beelzebub, Baal, the adversary, the deceiver, the prince of darkness, the prince of the power of the air, etc.

You may recall the account in *Luke Chapter 4* where Jesus is tempted by the devil.

> **The devil led him up to a high place and showed him in an instant all the kingdoms of the world.**
> **And he said to him 'I will give you all their authority and splendour, for it has been given to me and I can give it to anyone I want to'.** *Luke 4:5,6*

Let us look at this carefully. First it says that Satan showed Jesus all the kingdoms of the world in an instant. The devil must have a lot of power to be able to do this. Then he offered the authority of these kingdoms to Jesus and the splendour or glory that goes with the authority. How could he offer him this authority if he did not have it to give?

The truth is that Satan got the power and authority and

rulership of this domain when Adam transgressed in Eden. Because of his disobedience to God, Adam transferred the rulership over to Satan. In *II Corinthians 4:4* we are told that Satan is the 'God of this world'. This is why the world is in such a bad condition. He is the author of all the wars, famines, diseases, murders, rapes, etc., and it is Satan who has the power of death and sickness.

We can elicit another truth from the above quote from Luke. The devil said to Jesus 'all this authority I will give you ... I will give it to anyone I want to'. So who gave Hitler or Stalin their power? It is plain that the devil gave them their power and he will give it to you too if you want it badly enough. But you will pay the ultimate price.

Let us back track now and get a broader picture of who Satan is and where he came from. Originally there were three archangels created by God. Their names were Gabriel, Michael and Lucifer. The latter had the most power and was exceedingly beautiful and knowledgeable. 'Lucifer' means bearer of light. So he knows what light is and the secrets of light. Because of his wisdom and beauty, Lucifer became proud and wanted to be like the most high God and he tried to usurp the throne of God.

> **You were blameless in your ways from the day you were created till wickedness was found in you.**
> **Your heart became proud on account of your beauty, and you corrupted your wisdom because of your splendour.**
> **So I threw you to the earth ...** *Ezekiel 28:15,17*

A battle ensued in heaven and Lucifer was sent to earth. When he fell we are told that one-third of all the angels under his command sided with him and fell with him. So today Lucifer, or Satan, inhabits this earth with a vast multitude of fallen angels.

A reference is often made to the 'apple on the tree' and the 'snake' in the fall of Adam and Eve in *Genesis Chapter 3*. But there is no mention of an apple or of a snake in this record. What is described is a 'serpent' and a tree of the 'knowledge of good and evil'. The Hebrew word for serpent is *nachash* which means 'shining' or 'bright one' and infers a being of great wisdom, beauty and knowledge. Eve was deceived by this bright apparition. In *Corinthians 11:14* Satan is referred to as an 'Angel of Light' and this is what beguiled Eve. There is no mention of a snake or of an apple. But the majority of people have been deceived into thinking so.

We should also examine demon possession. The film, *The Exorcist,* is quite accurate biblically. Here is the biblical perspective:

> **They went across the lake to the region of the Gerasenes.**
> **When Jesus got out of the boat, a man with an evil spirit came from the tombs to meet Him.**
> **This man lived in the tombs and no one could bind him any more, not even with a chain.**
> **For he had often been chained hand and foot, but he tore the chains apart and broke the irons on his feet. No one was strong enough to subdue him.**
> **Night and day among the tombs and in the hills he would cry out and cut himself with stones.**
> **When he saw Jesus from a distance, he ran and fell on his knees in front of him. He shouted at the top of his voice, 'what do you want with me Jesus, Son of the most high God? Swear to God that you won't torture me!'**
> **For Jesus had said to him, 'Come out of this man you evil spirit.'**
> **Then Jesus asked him 'what is your name?'**
> **'My name is Legion,' he replied, 'for we are many'.**
> **And he begged Jesus again and again not to send them into the Abyss.**
> **A large herd of pigs was feeding on the nearby hillside. The demons begged Jesus 'send us among the pigs; allow us to go into them'.**
> **He gave them permission, and the evil spirits came out and went into the pigs. The herd, about two thousand in number, rushed down the steep bank into the lake and were drowned.**
>
> *Mark 5:1-13*

There are numerous accounts in the gospels of Jesus casting devil spirits or demons out of people who were possessed by them. Note in the above record that the demons knew exactly who Jesus was. They had no doubts of his divinity or of his authority or power. This man was possessed by a legion of demons. A Roman legion was about 6,000 men. They beseeched him not to cast them into the 'Abyss'. This is not the nearby water, but a place of detention for the evil angels that were responsible for the degradation and wickedness that led to the flood in the days of Noah.

We also see from this extract that Jesus Christ is the only one who can master these evil spirits and heal the individual. Later his disciples are given the power and authority to cast out devils in the name of Jesus. In *The Book of Acts* there are many instances of the Christians exorcising demons in the name of Jesus Christ.

Today there are still legions of demons possessing individuals and causing them to do vile acts of wickedness. This will increase as we draw closer to the Second Coming. During the seven years of Great Tribulation, these evil forces will be unleashed to a degree never witnessed before. They will cause destruction and mayhem on a global scale. Only the intervention of Jesus Christ will bring their reign of terror to a halt.

Thus far, we have seen the public face of the devil. But his main *modus operandi* is not demon possession but is much more subtle.

A cursory reading of the gospels shows that the antagonists to the preaching and teaching of Jesus were not demon-possessed people at all. No. The main enemy of the Word of God were the religious leaders of the day, the chief priests and the pharisees. Also the political rulers and the doctors of the law.

I was taught as a boy in school that it was Pontius Pilate who condemned Christ to be crucified. But this is wrong. The people who set him up were the ruling religious of the day.

As he taught Jesus said 'watch out for the teachers of the Law. They like to walk around in flowing robes and be greeted in the

> **market places,**
> **And have the most important seats in the synagogues and the places of honour at banquets.**
> **They devour widows' houses and for a show make lengthy prayers. Such men will be punished most severely'.**
>
> *Mark 12:38-40*

All through the Bible from the Old Testament to the New, anywhere a man of God was called to speak the Word of God, he invariably got his head chopped off by the religious or political leaders of the day. This is also true of Jesus.

> **Now the Passover and the feast of unleavened bread were only two days away, and the chief priests and the teachers of the law were looking for some sly way to arrest Jesus and kill him.**
>
> *Mark 14:1*

There are many such verses that could be quoted to illustrate the point. Almost every chapter in the gospels illustrates the hatred of the religious leaders of Jesus and their plotting to kill him. These were the bishops and theologians of the day. But these people did not deter the Son of God. Nor did Christ have problems dealing with them. In *John Chapter 8,* they were arguing with him and said that their father was God, to which Jesus replied:

> **Why do you not understand my speech? Because you cannot hear my word. You are of your father the devil, and the lusts of your father you will do. He was a murderer from the beginning, and abode not in the truth, because there is no truth in him.**
> **When he speaks a lie, he speaks of his own; for he is a liar and the father of it.** *John 8:43,44*

People think that, because you are a Christian you should be a door mat that they can wipe their feet on. But Jesus Christ was no door mat. He was a real man and he took no nonsense. Remember when he made a small whip from a rope and kicked over the tables of the money changers in the temple and drove them out? He was fearless and he confronted the religious leaders of the day head on. In the above passage, he accuses them of being the children of the devil. This is backed up by Paul later in Corinthians where he says:

> **But we speak the wisdom of God in a mystery ...**
> **Which none of the rulers of this world knew. For had they known it, they would not have crucified the Lord of Glory.**
> *I Corinthians 2:7,8*

We know that the main ruler of this world is Satan. He has his chain of command around him similar to the command structure of an army. He is the chief prince. Around him are his generals and colonels and lieutenants all the way down to privates. Paul tells us that had they known that, as a result of the death and resurrection of Jesus Christ now all men can be saved, they (the forces of evil), would never have crucified the Lord Jesus Christ.

Now we know that it was people who actually physically crucified him. But the spiritual forces who ordained it were Satan and his rulers who worked through these religious people to accomplish their ends.

Again we see this in Corinthians.

> **And no wonder, for Satan himself masquerades as an angel of light.**
> **It is not surprising then, if his servants masquerade as servants of righteousness.** *II Corinthians 11:14,15*

The chief priests and elders and Pharisees then, were servants of Satan and they appeared as servants of righteousness. In other words, these were people who were supposed to be teaching the ordinary people the way of God and the word of truth.

But Jesus said that they 'were of their father, the Devil'. That means that these religious leaders, in their flowing garb, were the children of the devil. He also said that 'the works of your father ye shall do'. Therefore what the religious leaders were perpetuating was lies, not the truth. And it is the same today. All the large so-called Christian religions say they represent the truth of God. But when you line it up with the teaching of Jesus, you soon see it is usually the direct opposite of what he taught. In other words, it is lies.

There is only one truth. Jesus said 'I am the way the truth and the life. No man comes to the father but by me', and so the devil does not want us to know the truth. He has his ministers, disguised as ministers of truth, feed us lies and deceptions based not on the truth of Scripture, but on the traditions and doctrines of men.

The only way you will be able to spot the counterfeit is if you know the truth. As Jesus said to the pharisees on another occasion:

> **You are blind leaders of the blind. And if the blind lead the blind, both shall fall into the ditch.**

Anything against the true interests of the Word of God finds a ready admission into the media of our day. But anything in favour of the Word of God, of its truth or divine inspiration, is rigidly excluded as being 'too controversial'.

The devil is the 'God of this world' and he is the one who is pulling the strings. Don't expect this book to get too much publicity.

The Marian Conspiracy

IF MARY, THE MOTHER of Jesus, knew what was being said and done in her name, she would be disgusted. If we profess to be Christians, then we must go back to the basis for our beliefs, Scripture, and allow it to speak for itself. Otherwise we may be in error in our doctrine and can end up believing in fables that bear no relation to what the Bible teaches. This is exactly what has happened in relation to Mary.

Let us go back to basics and examine the evidence. According to *Matthew Chapter 13*, Jesus had four brothers (or half brothers as we say) and at least three sisters. We pick up the story as he returns to his home town and begins preaching the good news.

> **Coming to his home town he began teaching the people and they were amazed.**
> **'Where did this man get this wisdom and these miraculous powers?' they asked.**
> **'Isn't this the carpenter's son?'**
> **'Isn't his mother's name Mary, and aren't his brothers, James, Joseph, Simon and Judas?'**
> **'Aren't all his sisters with us? Where did this man get all these things?'**
> **And they took offence at him.**
> **But Jesus said to them, 'Only in his home town and in his own**

> **house is a prophet without honour.'**
> **And he did not do many miracles there because of their lack of faith.** *Matthew 13: 53-58*

It is evident from this one quote alone that Jesus had four brothers and at least three sisters. These four brothers were only his half brothers in reality, for they were the sons and daughters of the marriage of Joseph and Mary. Jesus on the other hand, was the Son of God by divine conception.

The Lord is also called Mary's *'firstborn'* (*Matthew 1:25* and *Luke 2.7*) the inference being that, as he was born first, there were others born after him.

And why not? If we were to go by the culture of the time, then it is very likely that Mary was in her teens when she was found to be pregnant with her firstborn Jesus. She was already betrothed to Joseph at this time. We were often told that Joseph was already an old man. But there is no evidence for this in Scripture. In fact it is almost certain that Joseph was probably just a few years older than Mary, possibly a teenager himself, when all this took place. Joseph found himself in a dilemma when Mary was discovered to be pregnant, because he knew he wasn't the father. But an angel appeared to him and said '**be not afraid to take Mary home as your wife, because what is conceived in her is from the Holy Spirit**'.

So that is exactly what Joseph did, for he was a righteous man and he loved Mary. And consequently, when married, I am positive he made love to his wife and had a normal marital relationship. Thus Mary and Joseph had a family as their firstborn Jesus, grew up. We are not given much information about the earlier years but we are given some.

In other parts of the gospels, Christ's family are alluded to. For instance, after the miracle at the wedding in Cana, we are told:

> **'He went down to Capernaum, he and his mother and his brethren and his disciples.'** *John 2:12*

Religious teachers would have us believe that 'brethren' does not mean his family at all but has other connotations. The reason we are told this is because Mary has been raised from the position of '**Handmaid of the Lord**' (*Luke 1:38*) to the exalted one of *Theotokos*, meaning Mother of God, which does not appear anywhere in Scripture and is totally unbiblical. Thus being exalted to this high position of the mother of God, it was a small step to investing her with divine honours and making her a goddess in her own right. This only happened years after all the original apostles and disciples and indeed Mary herself were dead. When the doctrine began going away from the fundamentals of Scripture, beliefs and practices began infiltrating which were more common to pagan beliefs. Thus the ancient belief that a woman, who would be a virgin, would have a divine son and remain a virgin after the birth, crept into the church. This ancient pagan belief is quite common and best illustrated in the name she bore in Egypt where the great goddess Isis was the virgin mother of Horus.

Therefore we were taught that Mary was '*Blessed Mary, ever virgin*', that she never had sexual intercourse and she was without sin. Furthermore we were told that she never died but was '*assumed*' into heaven, where she now resides doing favours for all those who pray to her.

Mary was a wonderful young believer. It was she who accepted the responsibility of bearing the Messiah, Jesus, the Son of God. For this we are told that she would be ever-called 'Blessed' but that is it. She is no more or less exalted than anyone else in Scripture. Furthermore she died as did the rest of the first century believers and she is awaiting the second coming of her Son, Jesus, who will raise her from the dead on his appearing in the clouds.

The town of Ephesus in Turkey, where Paul spent two and a half years preaching the Word of God and from where Christianity spread in the early church, is close to the island of Patmos where John was imprisoned and where he wrote the

Apocalypse. There is a shrine there which is the house where Mary is believed to have died. When Jesus was dying on the cross he asked this same John to look after his mother. John was extremely close to Jesus. So the fact that Mary would have been in Ephesus when John was in Patmos is very likely. It is also interesting that the house where she died is still venerated, for if she died then she could not have been *assumed* into heaven. The reason we were told she was 'assumed' into heaven is because it is an 'assumption' and still the Roman Church has a day dedicated to this called the '*Assumption of Mary*'.

This is directly opposite to what Scripture teaches. It says when a person dies they stay dead until the resurrection. Mary and Joseph and their sons are all dead (or asleep according to the Bible) and are awaiting the second coming just like the rest of us. Furthermore, to pray to Mary for favours is incorrect according to Scripture. We are told specifically all through the New Testament to pray to God, the Father, in the name of his Son Jesus Christ, our Lord and Saviour.

> **For there is one God, and one mediator between God and men, the man Christ Jesus.** *I Timothy 2:5*

Remember what Jesus himself taught.

> **I am the way, the truth and the life. No man comes to the Father, except through me.** *Jesus Christ. John 14:6*

You cannot get to the Father any other way. You do not get to the Father by Mary, by the Pope, by your bishop or priest or anybody else, except through Jesus Christ.

Now you have a decision to make. You can believe what Jesus says or believe the doctrines and traditions of men. Put another way, if Jesus Christ says one thing and someone else tells you the opposite, who do you choose to believe? You can either believe the Son of God who was the Word made flesh, or you can believe the words of men. It is your choice. But there is only one truth. Have you ever read the first commandment in its entirety? It is recorded in *Exodus 20:*

> **I am the Lord your God ... You shall have no other Gods before me.**
> **You shall not make for yourself an idol in the form of anything in heaven above or on the earth beneath or in the waters below. You shall not bow down to them or worship them.**
> *Exodus 20: 1-5*

In the King James version of the Bible the word *'idol'* is a *'graven image'*. A graven image is a statue. Here in the very first commandment we are forbidden to have statues to anything from heaven to earth to the sea.

In the verse above these statues are called idols. Not only are we told not to have these idols but we are expressly forbidden to *'bow down to them, or worship them'*. Yet this is exactly what takes place in every Catholic Church.

According to the first commandment, this is idolatry. We are breaking the first commandment every time we kneel in front of a statue and pray to it, especially to statues of Mary or Joseph or Jude. This in not Christian, but idolatry based on paganism.

> **For I, the Lord your God, am a jealous God, punishing the children for the sin of the fathers to the third and fourth generation of those who hate me.**
> **But showing love to a thousand generations to those who love me and keep my commandments.** *Exodus 20:5,6*

Once you know the truth you are responsible for it. It is not our fault that we were wrongly taught. But it is our fault if we can read the truth in black and white and we still refuse to change.

All the mainstream Christian churches are steeped in idolatry and false teachings. Church Ministers regularly preach that virgin birth is a lie or the resurrection never really happened. Or they advocate the idea of homosexual marriage. Are we surprised? Not at all, for we are told in the epistles that one of the signs of the last days would be apostate Christian leaders teaching lies directly opposite to the truth of the Word of God.

> **And no wonder for Satan himself is transformed into an angel of light.**
> **It is not surprising then if his servants masquerade as servants of righteousness.**
> **Their end will be what their actions deserve.**
>
> *II Corinthians 11:14,15*

Is it not intriguing that the serpent that deceived Eve in the garden of Eden was not a snake at all. No, she held a conversation with a bright, fascinating angel of light which appeared to be full of wisdom and knowledge and beauty. She was tricked by a seemingly glorious celestial being whom she believed to be of superior aspect. Thus she was seduced by Satan himself.

It is no coincidence that when we study the details of the various appearances of Mary at Lourdes or Knock, or elsewhere, she always appears as a bright, shining, glorious being, full of grace and beauty. But it cannot be Mary who is making those visits because, according to God's Word, she is asleep (dead) waiting for Jesus to raise her up. So who is this glorious angel of light who is appearing in these places? It has to be Lucifer, the bearer of light, or one of his ministers who masquerade as angels of light.

If you do not know the revealed truth of the Word, you are always likely to be deceived by the deceiver. These apparitions of Mary, falsely so-called, are evidences of more lies from the father of lies.

The Ministry of Lies

A YOUNG PRIEST ONCE told me that the Church of Rome was founded on two precepts: (1) the Word of God and (2) the traditions of the church. Jesus in his earthly ministry was confronted for teaching against the Jewish traditions of the day.

> **Then came some pharisees and teachers of the law to Jesus from Jerusalem and asked, 'Why do your disciples break the tradition of the Elders?'**
> **Jesus replied, 'and why do you break the commandment of God for the sake of your tradition? You Hypocrites! Isaiah was right when he prophesied about you: These people come near to me with their mouth and honour me with their lips, but their hearts are far from me.**
> **They worship me in vain; their teachings are but rules taught by men.'** *Jesus Christ. Matthew 15: 1-3, 7-9*

Once again we see it is the religious people who are out to trap Jesus. In those days it was part of their religion that they wash their hands before eating. If they did not do so, they were sinning. Jesus threw the question right back at them saying *'why do you break the commandments of God by your traditions?'*

There is nothing in the Bible to suggest it was a commandment of God to wash your hands before eating. What the religious had done was made up their own laws and enforce these on the people. Then in time the traditions that are man made replace the Word of God and you are left with an empty doctrine which is purely of man's own making. Over time these religious people add more and more of their own doctrines which they say are based on the traditions of 'our forefathers'.

They may add some and drop some others as the fashion changes. So one day it was the truth, and had to be strictly observed, that you could not eat meat on a Friday. Now you can eat meat as much as you like. The Catholic Church is full of these contradictions. At the time they were the truth and everyone believed in them. Then, all of a sudden it is no longer the truth and another doctrine or tradition is put in its place.

This is exactly what Jesus was telling the priests and religious elders in this passage. They have taken the truth and replaced it with doctrines and traditions which are all man made. Earlier I mentioned the confrontation Jesus had with these same people who were plotting to kill him. His words must have cut into their hearts like knives when he said:

> **Ye are of your father the devil and the work of your father you will do. He is a liar and the father of lies.**
>
> *Jesus Christ. John 8:44*

Remember that he is referring to the chief priests and the Pharisees and the doctors of the law who he is dealing with. These are the people who got up in the pulpit every week to lecture the populace on how they ought to behave in order to please God.

But Jesus says that their work was to promote the product of their father which is *'lies'*. Has anything changed in 2,000 years? Absolutely not, for we are still being taught the same lies today dressed up as truth under the guise of the 'traditions of the church'. Truth does not change. It is absolute. The Word of God is the same. What was truth in Jesus' day is still true today. Remember the parable of the two men? One built his house upon the rock and the other built his house upon the sands.

When the storm and floods hit, the house that was built upon the sands was washed away but the house built on the rock was unmoved. All the large so-called Christian Churches are built on the traditions and doctrines of men.

When you line up what these churches are teaching beside what the Bible says, you find out that they are basically teaching lies. They are not representing the Father of Jesus Christ, but are working for their father who is the father of lies. So when men join these so-called Christian churches they spend years studying and become Ministers of Lies. Because their church is built on lies (sand), when the storms and floods of scandals arrive, the church begins to collapse. This is what is happening with the Catholic Church in Ireland today.

Another major scandal surrounding the church concerns the treatment of children in orphanages in the past – not only massive sexual abuse but also gross cruelty and allegedly even murder. And these were 'Christian' brothers. No. I say these were ministers of lies and servants of Satan.

At one point Jesus said: '**By their fruit will you know them**'. Judging by the revelations which have been emerging over the past few years we can see the fruit is rotten. Priests have been discovered in homosexual saunas and other seedy joints where complete strangers go to engage in illicit homosexual acts. So, for example, on Saturday evenings these Catholic priests are serving Mass and distributing communion, saying 'Thus saith the Lord'. Then they are indulging in vile sexual acts that night and the following morning they appear on the altar again, supposedly representing Jesus Christ! And still the people of Ireland bow down to them and kiss their ring. By their fruit you shall know them.

But also we are told by Paul that one of the signs of the end times would be so-called 'Christian' leaders teaching doctrines of devils and following deceiving spirits. This is the apostate church of the synagogue of Satan. And it is not just the Catholic church. You can now become a Methodist Minister and be openly homosexual, and this goes for many other Protestant churches all over the globe. Many of these ministers believe they are doing God's will. What a shock they are in for when they have to stand before the judgement seat of Christ.

> **Not everyone who says to me Lord, Lord, will enter, but only he who does the will of my father who is in heaven.**
> **Many will say to me on that day, Lord, Lord, did we not prophesy in your name, and in your name drive out demons and perform many miracles?**
> **Then I will tell them plainly, I never knew you. Away from me, you evildoers.** *Jesus Christ. Matthew 7:21-23*

The Word of God is the will of God. If you want to know his will then there is only one place you will find it. And that is in his Word. All you have to do is open it up and begin to read. Most of it is quite simple. If you need help you can go to a Christian bookshop which is full of good books and real Christian people who can advise you. When you build your faith on the Word of God, you are building on a rock.

> **For the Word of God is living and active. Sharper than any double edged sword, it penetrates even to dividing soul and spirit, joints and marrow: it judges the thoughts and attitudes of the heart.** *Hebrews 4:12*

That's how sharp and powerful God's Word is. Here is another example of the lies we are taught which emanated from the Ministry of Lies. One day his disciples came to him and asked Jesus how they should pray. His answered:

> **When you pray do not use vain repetition as the heathen do. For they think they will be heard because of their much speaking.**
> *Jesus Christ. Matthew 6:7*

What do you think the 'rosary is'? Repeating the 'Hail Mary' and the 'Our Father' over and over. This again is what we were taught to be truth. Yet it is opposite to what Christ said to do.

> **And do not call anyone on earth 'Father'. For you have one Father, and he is in heaven.** *Jesus Christ Matthew 23:9*

Here Jesus Christ commands us not to call any man 'Father'. Can he be any more specific? Now you are beginning to realise why our religious leaders do not want us to read the Bible. Many times in the Old Testament God is referred to as a rock which will provide us with shelter and protection. In the New Testament Jesus Christ is referred to as the chief cornerstone and the rock on which the true church is built upon. But we were taught that Peter is the rock and therefore the vicar of Christ for the world and the first Pope. We must examine exactly what Jesus said to determine the truth.

> **Thou art Peter and upon this rock I will build my church.**
> *Matthew 16:18*

In the Greek, Peter's name was *Petros* which literally means a small, moveable stone or even a grain of sand. But the Greek word used for rock is *Petra* meaning a big immovable rock. When Jesus made the above statement he was saying to Peter, look, you are a stone. One day you are standing by me, the next you are denying me and running away. 'But upon **this** rock (Petra), **I** will build **my** church. And the gates of hell (hades) will not prevail against it.' Jesus was talking about himself, for you cannot build a church upon a mere man as Peter was. Yes he was one of the twelve apostles and a great leader but he is not the rock. In fact we were told that he was the first Pope and Christ's vicar based upon the above passage, but we were never told about verse 23.

> **But he turned and said to Peter: 'Get thee behind me Satan: Thou art an offence unto me.'** *Matthew 16:23*

Peter is not the rock. The Pope is not Christ's vicar on earth. He is the leader of the Ministry of Lies. Jesus Christ is the Rock. The true Church of God consists of people who believe in Jesus

Christ and who have accepted him as their personal Lord and saviour. Jesus was not a Roman Catholic, neither were Mary nor the apostles or any of the first-century believers. It makes no difference to God whether you are a Catholic or a Protestant or a Moslem or a Jew. He does not care about what you have done in the past. He just wants you to know His love and become part of his family.

> **... And drank the same spiritual drink; For they drank from the spiritual rock that accompanied them, and that Rock was Christ.**
> *1 Corinthians 10:4*

There are only three types of people according to the Word of God. In the Old Testament the people of God were the children of Israel, later called Jews. Anybody else was a Gentile. When the Holy Spirit was given on the day of Pentecost and people received the Spirit of God when they believed, a third category of people came into existence, called the Church (*called out*) of God. Today we are called Christians. If you are a Christian, you are a member of the Body of Christ. He is the Head, we are members of his body. So, as far as God is concerned, you are either a Jew, Gentile or Church of God. All the other titles are man made. The word church in the Greek is *ekklesia* meaning '*called out*'. So the church of God is not a building or an edifice of some sort, but rather a group of people who have been '*called out*' from the rest. When Jesus Christ appears briefly in the clouds and all the Christians are caught away, we will all be the same. We will all have to appear before Christ Jesus to give an account of ourselves. And we will be rewarded if we have done well and used our talents.

Whether you are Catholic or not will not make a difference to God or his Son. That's why many will get a shock on that day. And that day is near. If you have not made a decision to put your trust in God and His Son, maybe now is the time. You do not want to be left behind.

On the other hand, if you are reading this and millions of

Christians have vanished, then you still have hope. But beware. If many of the religious leaders are still around after the Rapture, then be careful of what they say. If it does not agree with the truth of the Word, then you know that Satan is behind it. The first thing that will emerge after the Rapture is false Christs, false prophets and false messiahs. You have been warned.

> **Enter through the narrow gate. For wide is the gate and broad is the road that leads to destruction, and many enter through it. But small is the gate and narrow is the road that leads to life, and only a few find it.** *Jesus Christ. Matthew 7:13,14*

Trust in the Lord Jesus Christ. He is the Rock on which you can rely. All other belief systems are based upon the traditions and lies and belief systems of men. They are being swept away as the scandals and revelations continue to burst forth in flood and storm. But we have nothing to fear as we stand upon the Rock, await his soon return and our ticket away from '**the wrath to come**'.

The Legacy of the Inquisition

We have never been taught the history of the Popes and of the Roman Church. And for very good reason, for if ordinary people were exposed to the facts of the history of the Catholic Church, they would recoil in horror at the bloody events. The Inquisition is one such blot on the history of this anti-Christian church. Various Popes instituted this persecution of Protestants and other Christian groups. One such document that ordered the persecution was the *Ad Exstirpanda* issued by Pope Innocent IV in 1252. It ordered civil authorities to burn heretics and formally approved the use of torture. It became a fundamental document of the Inquisition and was reinforced by several Popes including Pope Alexander IV (1254-61), Pope Clement IV (1265-68), Pope Nicholas IV (1288-92), Pope Boniface VIII (1294-1303) and others. These Popes sanctioned and financed the mass torture and murder of other Christians who would not accept the authority of the Roman Church and of the Pope as being the vicar of Christ.

One of the favourite tools devised to produce the most pain was the 'rack'. People were tied hand and foot and then stretched until their joints dislocated. Heavy pincers were used to pull out fingernails or were applied red hot to sensitive parts of the body. Thumbscrews were used to dislocate fingers and

'Spanish boats' used to crush legs and feet. The infamous 'hallow virgin' was a life-sized metal dummy containing sharp spikes and blades. The 'heretic' was placed inside and the door closed so that the victim was impaled within. This device was blessed by holy water and inscribed in Latin with the words, 'Glory be only to God'.

In the year 1554, Francis Gamba, a Protestant, was condemned to death by the sentence of Milan. At the place of execution a Catholic monk presented a cross to him to which Gamba replied, 'My mind is so full of the real merits of Christ that I want not a piece of stick to put me in mind of him'. For this his tongue was bored through and he was afterwards burned. Some who rejected the teachings of the Roman Church as being incompatible with the teachings of Christ had molten lead poured into their ears and mouths. Eyes were gorged out and others beaten with whips. Others were choked to death with mangled pieces of their own bodies and with urine and excrement.

In 1209, in the city of Beziers, 60,000 were slaughtered as heretics by the Catholic inquisitors. At Lavaur in 1211, the inquisitors first attended high mass and then massacred 100,000 Albigenses (Protestants) in one day. Their bodies were heaped together and burned. Pope Pius IV sent the Italian army in 1562, to slay men, women and children in the massacre of Orange. 10,000 Huguenots (Protestants) were killed in Paris in 1572, on 'St Bartholomew's Day'. The papal court received the news with great rejoicing and Pope Gregory XIII went to mass to give thanks that so many heretics were slain. He ordered the papal mint to make coins commemorating the event with the words '*Ugonottorum Stranges 1572*' on them. This translated signifies, 'The Slaughter of the Huguenots 1572'. Many of these Huguenots fled and some settled in Ireland. Hence there is a Huguenot cemetery off St Stephen's Green in Dublin and an area in Cork city centre called the Huguenot Quarter.

The Inquisition was ordered by papal decree and confirmed

by Pope after Pope, and millions died. Can anyone really excuse this hideous expression of torture and hate? Who can defend these actions and believe that these people were acting on behalf of Christ and are infallible?

Northern Ireland

AS A CHILD I was raised to believe in the Roman Catholic faith. I served as an altar boy and the Christian Brothers taught me in secondary school. When I was aged 24, I had a 'Saul on the road to Damascus' conversion and became a Christian. For many years now I have been a student of the Bible and feel I can identify with both communities in Northern Ireland. I believe the outlook for the North is very bleak unless remedial action is taken.

As was pointed out in an earlier chapter, when Jesus spoke of the signs that would precede the seven years of Tribulation, He said, **'Nation will rise against nation and ethnic group against ethnic group'** *(Matthew 24:7)*. This is what has been happening in Northern Ireland for the past 30 years, with one ethnic tribe fighting against the other. During this time thousands of good people have suffered misery again and again at the hands of the murderers and 5,000 families have buried their sons and daughters.

But when the seven years of Great Tribulation begin to unfold, the last 30 years will be nothing in comparison to these final seven. When the protective hand of God is withdrawn from the earth, once the judgement begins to be poured out, all hell will break loose. There is potential for massive bloodshed in the North of Ireland, unless we can do something about it now.

There are many good Bible-believing Christians in Northern Ireland. Many of these people are doing their best to stand on the Word of the Lord and live the Christian life. It is clear that many of the Catholic community do not share this faith. This presents both a dilemma and an opportunity.

Many of the Catholics in Northern Ireland are good people. Even though they may have been taught many mistruths, many of them believe in God and in the resurrection of His son, Jesus Christ. So there is common ground among all who believe this truth. In the *Book of Romans*, Paul said that the Jews had a zeal for God, but it was not based on knowledge. In other words, they had a zeal or love for God but this was not based on a knowledge of the scriptures.

Many of the good Catholic and other people in the North are like this. Those people who have a good understanding of the Bible now have an opportunity. Should they keep well away from their ill-informed neighbour (be they Catholic or Protestant) or should they reach out with the gospel in an effort to help? What would Jesus Christ have you do?

This is a rhetorical question, for time and time again the Lord urges us to reach out with the Word in order to help those who are in need. There is certainly no point in burying your talents in the ground.

As I already pointed out, there are only three types of people in God's eyes – Jew, Gentile and Church of God. There is no Church of England, Free Presbyterian or Roman Catholic with Him, only those who are saved, and those people waiting to be saved. He has no hands but our hands, no mouth but our mouth. It is up to us to reach out with the truth to those who need it. We must go to our neighbour as a representative of Jesus Christ and not as representing one denomination or another.

As Christians with a knowledge of scripture and an assurance of our salvation, we also need to end the haggling among ourselves. Too many Christians spend too much time arguing over petty differences rather than agreeing on the important major issues. One group believes in one thing, so they will not join us in fellowship with another Christian group who disagree with them. When Christians get together they are usually at each other's throats within minutes over their theological differences. Most of these issues are not important to God at all. If you want to know what is important to God and what is not, then let the Bible tell you. Do you know what is important? Unity among all Christians, that is what is imporant.

> **I appeal to you, brothers, in the name of our Lord Jesus Christ, that all of you agree with one another so that there may be no divisions among you.** *I Corinthians 1:10*

As a spiritual person, one should know that this is what we should be striving for. If something is so important, then surely God would write a whole chapter on it, don't you think? Well *1 Corinthians 13* is a whole chapter on love. Maybe Christians should spend more time on developing this aspect of their walk with God rather than fighting with their fellow Christians about whether or not six angels can dance on the head of a pin. You know that what the Lord said would happen, will absolutely happen. The devil has had a field day in your country for the past 30 years and he is licking his lips like the proverbial wolf at the prospect of what may be. It is up to you to do something now to help avoid the possible massacre of the innocents on both sides. It is up to you to reach out.

All those who say they believe in Jesus Christ are in the same boat, for He is *'the way the truth and the life'*. Your only hope is through Him. It matters not what any Priest or Bishop or Pope or Protestant Archbishop or what anybody else says. Our only hope and your country's only hope is through Jesus Christ. Unless you realise this and come together under the one banner of the Lord, the streets of Northern Ireland will flow with the blood of men, women and children. This is what Jesus Christ is telling us in *Matthew 24*.

There are hard line bigots on both sides who despise and hate those of other religions. But you must realise that it is Satan who is behind violence and murder. He is the author of death (*Hebrews 2:14*). Anybody who commits murder cannot have eternal life and the people who perpetrate hatred and violence are instruments of the devil, whether they are Protestant or Catholic. Little do these people realise that for their sins they will be spending a long time together when the Lord comes to judge them, for although they believe they are fighting for a cause, they are actually working for the same boss. Satan is the one who is pulling the strings. The terrorists on both sides are supping with the devil using a very short spoon.

Could anyone find fault with the Christian love displayed by Mr Gordon Wilson after his own daughter was murdered? He almost immediately forgave those who carried out the deed. This is what Jesus told his disciples to do. Forgive those who sin against you and do you harm. Gordon Wilson is an example of a good Christian who not only knew the Bible, but acted out what it said to do.

For the sake of your children, you must forgive and forget the past. Unless you understand the prophecies of Jesus Christ and realise that they shall absolutely come to pass, many will die.

In conclusion, perhaps both groups should look to St Patrick for inspiration. It is clear that he was a Christian who preached the Word of God. His letters are peppered with quotes from scripture showing that Patrick knew his Bible. He was a great Christian teacher who converted many of the Irish pagans to Jesus Christ. He was persecuted by the chieftains and the Picts and many of his young Christian converts were tortured and killed for their faith.

So our heritage, from the Golden Age of Ireland, is a Christian one based on the literal teachings of scripture. During this Golden Age, many Irish men went throughout Europe preaching the *'Word of Christ'*. History tells us that it took the religious authorities about 100 years to change Ireland from its old form of Christianity, as taught by Patrick, over to Roman Catholicism. Prior to this, our heritage was that of a Christian nature based on the teachings of the Word of God. This is the reason Ireland was known as the Land of Saints and Scholars. Perhaps we should return to St Patrick's way of thinking.

God is no respecter of persons. He wants all men to be saved and to come to a knowledge of the truth. He gave His son to death so that you and I might have life. When we get to Paradise, we will all be one in Christ Jesus, for there is one God, one baptism, one church and one Lord who is over us all. Politicians, Ministers and other dignatories will never deliver peace in Northern Ireland. All they are doing is rearranging the deck chairs on the *Titanic*. There will be no peace until we return to the *Prince of Peace*, Jesus Christ, and the author of peace, God. May God and Jesus grant you peace.

Born from Above

Not all the religious leaders in the days of Christ were totally blind. Some realised who He was.

> **Now there was a man of the Pharisees named Nicodemus, a member of the ruling Jewish council.**
> **He came to Jesus at night and said 'Rabbi, we know you are a teacher come from God for no one could do the miraculous signs that you are doing if God were not with him'.**
> **In reply Jesus declared, 'I tell you the truth, no one can see the kingdom of God unless he is born again'.**
> **'How can a man be born when he is old?' Nicodemus asked. 'Surely he cannot enter a second time into his mother's womb to be born,' Jesus answered, ' I tell you the truth, no one can enter the kingdom of God unless he is born of water and the spirit. Flesh gives birth to flesh, but the spirit gives birth to spirit.'**
>
> *John 3:1-6*

The first unusual thing we notice in this passage is that Nicodemus came to Jesus at night. He did not want to be seen talking with Jesus, for he was a member of the Sanhedrin, the ruling religious leaders who were opposed to Jesus. Had he been caught, he might well have been ostracised and lost the prestige and remuneration of his position.

But Jesus ignored his opening statement and replied with a

startling pronouncement. *'Unless a man is born again he* ***cannot*** *enter the kingdom of God'*. The Greek work for 'Born Again' is *another* which literally means, 'Born from Above'. That is, by divine power. Nicodemus misunderstands Jesus who then elaborates. The flesh gives birth to flesh, but the Spirit gives birth to Spirit. In other words, the first time you are born, the seed from your father fertilises the egg in your mother. Nine months later the baby is born for flesh gives birth to flesh. But when you are born from above it is a spiritual rebirth. The seed from God is spirit. It comes down from above, meaning the spirit is sent from God into our hearts. Once we receive this spirit we cannot lose it for it is incorruptible seed.

> **Being born again not of corruptible seed but of incorruptible, by the Word of God which lives and abides forever.** *I Peter 1:23*

Because this seed is from God it cannot be corrupted and it cannot perish. Just as you cannot be unborn, so too you cannot lose the spiritual seed once you have received it. You may abuse your new status as a child of God and never walk in the truth, but you cannot lose the spirit because it is the seed from God. In fact, unless you are born again you cannot enter the kingdom of God. Yet were we ever told we had to be born again? No. We were told we must be baptised. But you can pour water on someone's head forever, yet it will not get you into the kingdom of God. How do you get born again? Simple. According to this last verse quoted, we are born again by the Word of God. In other words, when you hear a certain amount of the Word, you reach a point where you have heard enough evidence to cause you to believe the promise of salvation through the redeeming work of Christ. Once you have reached this point all you have to do is written in *Romans*.

> **That if you confess with you mouth 'Jesus is Lord' and believe in your heart that God raised him from the dead, you will be saved.**

> **For it is with your heart that you believe and are justified, and it is with your mouth that you confess and are saved.**
>
> *Romans 10:9,10*

This is all there is to it. You can do this right now. Because when you know the truth, you are set free.

> **Then you will know the truth and the truth shall set you free.**
>
> *Jesus Christ. John 8:32*

So many people are in bondage today. Yet we are promised by Jesus Christ Himself that if we come to Him with an open heart, He will set us free. And not only free in this life, but also eternal freedom from death and also eternal life. *John 3:16* is one of the most well known of all verses.

> **God so loved the world that He gave His only begotten Son, that whosoever believes in Him should not perish but have everlasting life.**
>
> *Jesus Christ*

This is a free gift from God. You cannot earn it for it is given by grace. Grace means 'Divine Favour'. You have been favoured by God and can receive His spirit and thus be born from above. When you make this decision you join the family of God. You are going to heaven and all hell cannot stop you from getting there.

> **But as many as received Him, to them he gave power to become the children of God, even to them that believe in his name.**
>
> *John 1:12*

What an incredible privilege. There are thousands and millions that have come and gone and never knew God. When you receive the gift of the Holy Spirit, you have eternal life abiding within you. You are now God's child.

> **How great is the love the Father has lavished on us, that we should be called children of God. And that is what we are.**

> **Dear friends, now we are children of God, and what we will be has not yet been made known. But we know that when He appears, we shall be like Him, for we shall see Him as he is.**
>
> *I John 3:1,2*

And that day when we shall see Him face to face may not be so far off. If you are still undecided, then what you need to do is read the Word of God. Then just listen to what it says, for it has the power to change your life. *Matthew 7:7* says **'ask and it shall be given; seek and you shall find; knock and the door shall be opened'**. If you go up to a door and just stand outside without knocking, you will not get in. So when you read your Bible, ask God to open your eyes and guide you.

> **Come unto me all you that labour and are heavy laden and I will give you rest. Take my yoke upon you and learn from me; for I am meek and lowly in heart: and you shall find rest unto your souls. For my yoke is easy and my burden is light.**
>
> *Jesus Christ. Matthew 11:28-30*

It is amazing what a comfort you will receive by just reading the words of God, for these are the words of life. Today we are surrounded by so much doubt and uncertainty. Violence and fear surround us. Despair and chaos are everywhere. But the Word of God is a sure rock that we can anchor to.

> **The spirit gives life; the flesh counts for nothing. The words I have spoken to you are spirit, and they are life.**
>
> *Jesus Christ. John 6:63*

Is Anybody Out There?

Is there intelligent life on other planets? This is a question that is debated a lot these days in forums all over the world. Many believe that because there are billions of planets and stars and other galaxies, then, by mathematical probability, there has to be other intelligent life out there somewhere. We are even sending out radio waves into space hoping that they will be received and responded to. Let us see what the Bible says about this subject.

In His risen body, Jesus Christ was the same man as before His death but He had extra dimensions to His new spiritual body. For instance in His risen state He could disappear as He did after walking the eight miles with the two disciples on the road to Emmaus. Another time He appeared in a room full of the apostles. But He was still the same person as before. We know this because doubting Thomas would not believe that Jesus was resurrected until he felt the holes in His hands and put his finger into the hole in His side. A week later, Jesus appeared to him and the others, and invited Thomas to touch Him saying 'I am not a ghost'.

In *John 21* Jesus cooked and ate fish with Peter and some of the other disciples. He also ate bread and honey and at the last supper He told His apostles, **'I will not drink of the fruit of the**

vine, until I am with you in Paradise'.

We are informed in the Epistles that when we are 'caught away' at the Rapture we will receive a new spiritual body like Jesus has. But as He ate fish and bread and promised that He would drink wine again, so too in our new spiritual bodies, we will be able to enjoy the delights of eating and drinking. When Jesus was still with His disciples on this earth, He told them:

> **In my father's house are many rooms:**
> **If it were not so I would have told you.**
> **I am going to prepare a place for you.**
> **And if I go and prepare a place for you I will come back and take you to be with me.**
> **That you also may be where I am.** *Jesus Christ, John 14:2,3*

So He is right now in this place called 'Heaven' where He is preparing a place for us. When He comes to take us out we will be changed in the *'twinkling of an eye'*, (*I Corinthians 15:52*) in a flash, and we will meet Him in the clouds, and from there we will be 'spirited' to Heaven. We are informed that residing in this place is God the Father. Seated on His right hand is His Son, Christ Jesus. Always when the victorious risen Christ is spoken of, He is referred to as Christ Jesus and not Jesus Christ who was tortured and died. However, along with God on His throne and His Son on His right hand, we have 24 elders who are spoken of in *Revelation*. And also in this heaven we have an innumerable amount of spirit beings known as 'angels'.

The Greek word for angel is *aggelos* which literally means 'messenger' or 'agent'. These are often called men in the Bible, as in the record where two 'agents' or 'messengers' are sent in to Sodom and Gomorrah to get Lot and his family out before the place is destroyed. Lot invited them into his house, washed their feet and made them a meal. Both young and old wanted to have sex with them so they were obviosuly attractive. So these spirit men, although they are angels, are not sexless. (There is only one mention of female angels in the whole Bible and that is in *Zechariah 5*). These spirit men are created beings and have no need for procreation although we know that they have the power to do so. According to the record in *Genesis 6:1-4* where we are told the 'Sons of God' (fallen angels) had sexual intercourse with the daughters of men and produced these half-demon, half-human giants who were exceedingly evil and wicked and were responsible for the degradation that brought on the flood in the days of Noah. These same wicked angels are reserved in the underworld according to *Jude 6* and *2 Peter 2:4,* and are awaiting judgement.

These messengers or agents of God appear many times throughout the Old and New Testaments. They ministered to Jesus after His temptation in the desert. It was Gabriel who told Mary that she would bear a son, for he seems to be the one who delivers messages. When Jesus hung on the cross, He said He had twelve legions of spirit men at His disposal if He needed them. A Roman legion was 6,000 men. So he had 72,000 ready to come to His aid if He so wished.

When Jesus ascended from the Mount of Olives two men appeared to the apostles and said to them:

> **You men of Galilee, why do you stand here looking up into heaven? This same Jesus, which is taken up from you into heaven, shall so come in like manner as you have seen him go into heaven.** *Acts 1:10,11*

These two men were probably Gabriel and Michael, the two archangels who have very high stations in God's hierarchy. According to *Luke 20:36,* angels cannot die. We do have guardian angels who protect us from evil. At one time during the gospels, a group of children came to Jesus and the disciples tried to chase them away. But Jesus told them to leave the children alone. He said the kingdom of heaven will be full of people who are like children. He also said that their (the children's) angels appear daily in the presence of God and see His face (*Matthew 18:10*). Interestingly, in this one passage talking about children, Jesus says if anyone causes a little child to sin, it would be better if a millstone was tied around his neck and he was drowned in the depth of the sea. I have not heard any of the bishops advocating this scripture when discussing the sexual abuse of children by the clergy! We are told that we should, as Christians, be forgiving and show mercy. But yet Jesus Himself said it would be better for these people if they were drowned. Who are we to contradict Jesus?

We have learned already that when Lucifer fell he brought one third of all the angels who sided with him. These invisible spirits inhabit the earth and are the cause of all the evil and sin that prevails in the world today. They are the 'deceiving' spirits who will trick all the nations of the globe finally bringing on the conflagration that will result in the death of 3 billion people by the end of the seven years of Great Tribulation. They are called 'familiar spirits' in the Old Testament. These are the spirits that operate through mediums and fortune tellers and seances and ouija boards and all the other occult and black arts. When someone hears a dead relative speak to them through a medium, telling them something that only the two of them know, it is not their dead communicating with them. Rather it is a 'familiar spirit', an evil spirit operating through the medium in order to deceive and lead people down the wrong road. These spirits can tell of things that only you and the dead person knew of because, as spirits, they have been around since time began. They know all you did during your life, and this is why they are called 'familiar spirits'. So do not be deceived – all the so-called occult art, from black and white magic to Tarot cards to palm reading are all operated by evil spirits.

It is these same fallen angels that work through the so-called 'religious' of our day. They are out to deceive and this is why they are called 'deceiving spirits' in *II Timothy 4:1*. As Lucifer means **'Bearer of Light'**, he knows how to appear as an apostle of light. And no wonder, for Satan himself masquerades as an angel of light. It is not surprising then if his servants masquerade as servants of righteousness *(II Corinthians 11:14,15).*

So, just because someone stands up in a pulpit with a Bible under his arm, this does not mean that he represents God or Jesus and that he speaks the truth. Unless you can document line by line and verse by verse what the truth says, you will always be deceived and be in error.

All the secrets you need to know are already revealed in the scriptures. And they are revealed by the Son of God, Jesus Christ, not by Mary or anyone else. If you do not know your Bible then the devil will trick you and lead you down the wrong path every time. Unless you come to the light, you will always be in darkness. Another phenomenon that Jesus told us to watch out for in the last days is **'fearful sights and great signs shall there be from heaven'** (*Luke 21:11*). The 'heavens' biblically can refer to the atmosphere around the earth or space as opposed to the place where Jesus is right now. Very often today we hear of strange objects being seen by pilots of planes and others who identify them as UFOs. Many people claim they have been abducted by these strange aliens and subjected to examinations. Consequently people believe that these are aliens from another planet and that they are of higher intelligence than we are. So why don't they land and introduce themselves? The reason they won't do this is because they are not benign benevolent aliens come to help us. No, I believe these are just another manifestation of the fallen angels of Lucifer, come to deceive in another form.

So when the world press ask the question, is there life on other planets? The answer is yes! Jesus is there preparing a place for us. His Father is there as are the 24 elders and millions upon millions of spirit beings who are men but we call angels. It must be a big place if all these beings are living there and if it has to facilitate all the Christians who have lived and died in the last 2,000 years. But heaven exists. We are going there for seven years at least while the horrible events of the Tribulation are played out.

The Septa Millennial Theory

We have covered many aspects of the events that are to occur in the near future. If you would like to be more clear on the order of these, I suggest you go back to Chapter 5 which gives the order and a summary of the things to come. But the first major event that must happen before anything else is the return of the Lord and our gathering together to be with Him.

I do not know exactly when the Lord is coming back. We are strictly forbidden to fix dates. However, we are told that we can know the general time of His second coming by the description of the conditions of the end times given to us in scripture. Thus we have examined many of the prophesies concerning the 'last days' and they would suggest that we are indeed very close to the second coming of Christ and the Rapture of the saints. Here is a brief review of the signs of the times. You will witness many of these things happening as we draw closer to the day. What to watch out for:

1. Increase in deception.
2. False Christs and false prophets.
3. Wars and rumours of wars: ethnic group against ethnic group.
4. Increase in famines, earthquakes, diseases.

5. Increase in peculiar weather patterns, storms.
6. Restoration of Israel to Palestine.
7. Rise in power of the 'King of the North', Russia.
8. Formation of the revived Roman Empire (the EU).
9. Rise in power and influence of Moslem nations.
10. Rise in power and influence of China and the countries of the East.
11. Increase in knowledge of the last days.
12. Racial intolerance and persecution of Christians.
13. Apostasy: turning away from God and Christian morals.
14. Men becoming lovers of themselves, lovers of money, lovers of pleasure.
15. Increase of scoffers.
16. Rise of spiritualism.
17. Increase in sexual immorality.
18. With the increase in wickedness, the love of many will grow cold.
19. It will become an age of abundance of food and appetite.
20. Abundance of idleness.
21. Abundance of business and commercialism.
22. With the increase in liberal views, violence will also increase.

Jesus Christ warned us that the world will get progressively worse until the final judgements will fall and will culminate in Armageddon at the end of the seven years of Tribulation. One theory that would seem plausible as to the timing of this final period, is called the 'Septa Millennial Theory'. This is based upon a verse in *II Peter 3:8.*

> **With the Lord, a day is like a thousand years, and a thousand years are like a day.**

In *Genesis,* God created the earth as we know it today, in six days and then rested on the seventh day. This seventh day was called the Sabbath. Man was to do no work on the Sabbath but to rest and enjoy what God had provided for him. There are 4,000 years separating Adam and Jesus Christ. From the time of Jesus to now is almost 2,000 years making a total of 6,000 years from Adam to now. Thus we know that the next 1,000 years will be a blessed time of real peace and prosperity under the rulership of Christ. Based on the above verse where 1,000 years is like a day and a day is like 1,000 years, we have almost completed six days, the seventh day being the Sabbath, the day of rest. Thus the first 6,000 years represent the six days of creation and the final 1,000 years in Paradise represent the seventh day of rest. If this theory is correct, and many observers believe it is, then we are close to the end of the 6,000 years right now which means that the Rapture of the believers, the saints of God, is imminent. Just how close, we do not know. But when it does occur it must be followed by the Great Tribulation, which is to last for seven years after the Antichrist signs a peace deal between Israel and her enemies. Then, at the close of the seven years and after the great war which begins at Armageddon, the Lord Jesus will return to the Mount of Olives with great power and glory, to begin his 1,000-year reign on earth.

I would like to say a little here about the expression 'the Saints of God'. This expression is found throughout the Old and New Testaments and throughout *The Book of Revelation*. It always refers to the people of God: to His people who trust in Him, and whom He owns. The word 'saint' literally means 'separated one' or 'holy one'. When you believe in Jesus Christ, when you have personally accepted him as your Lord and Saviour, you are then saved and that means you are separated from the rest of mankind and God has made you 'holy' as a result. It is nothing to do with your works as a person. But it has a lot to do with the grace of God. So the 'saints' of the New Testament days of the first century were just ordinary people who accepted Jesus Christ and who were saved thereby. This is why all the Epistles are addressed to the saints at Rome ... the saints at Ephesus ... the saints at Collosse and at Phillipi and so on.

People who believe in Christ today are called Christians. But most people in the Western Hemisphere think they are Christians, but they are not. To be a real Christian you must believe in Jesus Christ and you must be 'born again' or 'born from above' of God's Spirit. When you have God's Holy Spirit abiding in you, then you are a 'saint'. By the same token, the word 'church' in the Epistles does not mean a building where people gather. The Greek word for *church* is *Ekklesia* meaning *'called out'*. Those of us who believe are *'called out'* and separated from the rest of the people who do not believe. Thus the 'church of God' are the *'called out of God'*. So when you read Paul's Epistles, they are addressed to the Church (*called out*) at Rome ... the church (called out) at Corinth, the church (*called out)* at Galatia, etc. This is why Paul pointed out that there are only three types of people in God's eyes: the Jews, the Gentiles and the Church of God. So right now your are either a Jew, and if you are not a Jew, you are a Gentile. And if you have accepted Jesus as your personal Lord and Saviour, you have become one of the Church *(called out)* of God.

Being a saint of God, therefore, has absolutely nothing to do with the teachings of the Roman Church which are based on traditions and doctrines of men. This is why all through the Bible you will read of the 'saints of God' as referring to His children, His family.

Europe in Prophecy

NEBUCHADNEZZAR WAS THE KING and ruler of the Babylonian Empire about 2,500 years ago. The prophet Daniel had risen to a position of authority in Nebuchadnezzar's government because of his knowledge and learning. He and the Jewish nation were in captivity in the Babylonian Empire at that time. The king had a dream one night that greatly troubled him. He called for his advisers to interpret this dream. He would not tell them what the dream was because he did not want them to fabricate an interpretation. They had to tell him what the dream was and then give the meaning of it. His advisers, magicians, sorcerers and astrologers could not tell him what his dream was, let alone give him the meaning of it. At this, Nebuchadnezzar was upset and ordered all the wise men of Babylon to be executed. Daniel stepped in and offered the emperor an alternative solution. He said that if he could tell the king his dream and give him the meaning of it, then the lives of all the wise men of Babylon should be spared. The king agreed.

Daniel prayed to God for the details of the dream and the interpretation. He then went to Nebuchadnezzar and told him that only God can reveal mysteries of things to come and give interpretations of dreams.

> **You looked, O King, and there before you stood a large statue – an enormous, dazzling statue, awesome in appearance. The head of the statue was made of pure gold, its chest and arms of silver, its belly and thighs of bronze, its legs of iron, its feet partly in iron and partly of baked clay. While you were watching, a rock was cut out, but not by human hands. It struck the statue on its feet of iron and clay and smashed them. Then the iron, the clay, the bronze, the silver and the gold were broken to pieces at the same time and became like chaff on the threshing floor in summer. The wind swept them away without leaving a trace. But the rock that struck the statue became a huge mountain and filled the whole earth.**
> *Daniel 2:31-35*

The king was amazed at the accuracy of the details of his dream. Daniel then went on to give the interpretation of the statue the king had seen and the meaning thereof. Daniel told the king that the four parts of the statue represented four mighty kingdoms that would rule the world. The first kingdom was the Babylonian Empire and Nebuchadnezzar was the first ruler – **'You are the head of gold'**. Daniel then went on to explain that the other three parts were kingdoms that would rule the world in future years. The arms of silver represented the Medo-Persian Empire that conquered Babylon only a few years later. The thighs of bronze represented the Greek Empire which subsequently controlled most of the then known world under Alexander the Great. Finally, Daniel describes a fourth kingdom in verses 40-44. This prophecy is only partially fulfilled and therefore awaits complete fulfilment. This fourth kingdom is the Roman Empire. The iron heel of Rome ruled for many centuries until it collapsed because of decadence. Daniel spoke of the statue having feet of iron mixed with clay and he said that a huge rock would finally smash the feet and turn the whole statue to dust. This rock is of course Jesus Christ. When He returns He will establish His Kingdom where God's will will be done on earth as it is in heaven. Many scholars believe that the clay is democracy and that mixed together with iron represents the old

Roman Empire revived. This Empire, however, would co-exist by voluntary union and not by military conquest.

Now look at another vision received by *Daniel* in chapter 7. Here he sees the same four kingdoms, but this time they are called 'beasts'. The last beast is Rome which is described as mighty and powerful, devouring everything in its march. Now observe this prophecy:

> **The ten horns are ten kings who will come from this kingdom. After them another king will arise, differing from the earlier ones; he will subdue three kings. He will speak against the Most High and oppress his saints and try to change the set times and the laws. The saints will be handed over to him for a time, times and half a time.** *Daniel 7:24-25*

Here we have a confederacy of ten nations. The Antichrist will put down three nations and will persecute the saints and speak blasphemy against the Most High. This is corroborated in 2 *Thessalonians 2:3-4* and in *Revelation 17:12-13.*

> **The ten horns you saw are ten kings who have not yet received a kingdom, but who for one hour will receive authority as kings along with the beast.**
> **They have one purpose and will give their power and authority to the beast.**

This prophecy says that in the Tribulation period a ten nation confederacy will emerge. These ten nations will give authority and power to the beast who is the Antichrist. The European Union has arisen by voluntary agreement from the ashes of the old Roman Empire. Many commentators believe that the EU is the basis for this ten-nation confederacy that will virtually rule the world under the leadership of the Antichrist. However, judging by the way political allegiances are emerging at present, I would suggest that perhaps this future union would be made up of a Western-led alliance of rich nations whose roots go back to the Roman Empire. Thus this future alliance would resemble something like the present union of wealthy nations known as the G8. Therefore this future alliance would be made up of powerful European nations plus the United States and Canada and some other wealthy nations.

As already pointed out, as far as we can deduce nuclear war will erupt at the final battle. Any country who is aligned with the Antichrist will be an obvious target for enemy nuclear weapons. We are told that after the *'flashes of light, rumblings, peals of thunder ... then a huge earthquake, and the cities of the world collapse'*. If Ireland is still in the EU and this is the confederacy that is headed up by the Antichrist, then Dublin and Belfast will be targets in a nuclear attack. Provision must be made for the ensuing years of famine and scarcity of water that will ravage the world. The people who turn to God and Jesus Christ for refuge during the Great Tribulation are going to experience great hardship and persecution. As long as we know what lies ahead we have the opportunity to do something about it. Trust in God and in His son the Lord Jesus Christ and your eternal future will be secured.

Shall Never Perish

IF YOU HAVE REACHED this far in this book, you will have learned many things. The most important will pertain to your own situation. I would like to relate to you now a few verses from scripture which I hope you will enjoy.

> **My sheep hear my voice and I know them and they follow me: and I give unto them eternal life; and they shall never perish; neither shall any man pluck them out of my hand.**
> **My Father who gave them unto me, is greater than all; and no one is able to snatch them out of my Father's hand.**
>
> *Jesus Christ. John 10:27-29*

This is a fantastic assurance to those of us who believe the promise of Jesus. For once you accept His Word, you can never again be in fear of losing your eternal life. The best-known scripture in the Bible is probably *John 3:16:*

> **For God so loved the world, he gave his only begotten son that whosoever believes in him should not perish but have everlasting life.** *Jesus Christ. John 3:16*

There is no great mystery attached to getting saved. All you simply have to do is accept that Jesus died for you and rose again. You do not need to do any works or penance to get salvation. Just believe in the finished work of Jesus Christ and believe God raised Him from the dead.

> **That if you confess with your mouth 'Jesus is Lord' and believe in your heart that God raised him from the dead, you will be saved.**
> **For it is with your heart that you believe and are justified, and it is with your mouth that you confess and are saved.**
>
> *Romans 10:9,10*

You can do this anywhere and at anytime. You can be lying in your bed or walking in the woods. The important thing is that you do it. You confess Jesus as Lord and you believe that God raised Him from the dead. Once you do this, you get the gift of the Holy Spirit and you become a child of God. You are now going to heaven when Jesus comes back, for when you receive the gift of the Holy Spirit, you receive the seed of God and you are now born of His seed. You cannot be 'unborn' of His seed anymore than you can be unborn of your natural father's seed. If you want to learn more, then I suggest you get a Bible and just start reading and listening to what it says. A good rule to follow each time you go to the Bible is the following:

> **Ask and it will be given you: seek and you will find; knock and the door will be opened to you.** *Jesus Christ. Matthew 7:7*

When you apply this principle, God will open your eyes and thrill your heart as you read. This will be a great comfort to you in these dark days as we wait for His Son from heaven who is coming back to rescue us from the wrath to come.

> **Listen, I tell you a mystery: we will not all sleep, but we will all be changed.**
> **In a flash, in the twinkling of an eye, at the last trumpet. For the trumpet will sound, the dead will be raised imperishable, and we will be changed.** *I Corinthians 15:51,52*

> **For the Lord himself will come down from heaven, with a loud command, with the voice of the archangel and with the trumpet call of God, and the dead in Christ will rise first.**
> **After that, we who are still alive and are left will be caught up together with them in the clouds to meet the Lord in the air. And**

> **so will we be with the Lord forever.**
> **Therefore, encourage each other with these words.**
> *I Thessalonians 4:16-18*

Did you know that the original Christians in the first century were so sure the Lord was coming back, that when they got home from work they used to go up on their flat roofs to wait for Him? Well, we are 2,000 years further down the road and we are still waiting. But we are close to His second coming. In the meantime we can encourage one another.

On the other hand, I am sure that many people you know do not believe and are not really interested in what you have to say. When we are 'caught away' at the Rapture, many of our loved ones will be left behind. So what can you do in the meantime? Well, for a start, if you have read this book and you believe it helped you, you can give it to other people to read so that they may be blessed reading it. This book will do no good if it is not being read. Even people who are not interested right now may change very fast when they witness the disappearance of millions of believers. These people also need to know what is going to happen so they will be able to take action when the time comes. They need to have this book available to them. *Apocalypse 2000* can be a legacy to those who are left behind after the Rapture. This book can be a legacy to those who are left behind.

Once the Great Tribulation has taken place, there will be famine on the earth and one-third of all drinking water will be polluted. So you must plan to have food to eat and water to drink. There will be a global economic collapse also. But if you want to live to see the face of Jesus Christ, you must put your faith in Him. The Great Tribulation will last seven years. Do not succumb to the threats of the Antichrist. There will be many who turn to God and His son in these last days. Work together with them and call on the Lord for help. We have told you what is going to happen so that you might know. May God Bless you.